REUNITING WITH THE RANCHER

THE SILVER CREEK RANCH
BOOK 4

TERREECE M CLARKE

LIFESLICE MEDIA

The Silver Creek Ranch

Forgotten military heroes who needed a helping hand re-entering the society they had been sworn to protect. The Silver Creek Ranch provided a space where these cowboys could work the land and get back in touch with the men they once were.

The battles of war left scars on each of them.

Healing was what these cowboys needed.

Who knew it would comprise the touch, kiss, and love of a good woman?

The Silver Creek Ranch is an interracial cowboy romance shared world. Each captivating story is filled with plenty of heat and will leave your heart racing with the desire to devour every one of them.

When fate reunites a wounded warrior and a pop sensation sparks fly, secrets are revealed, and love heals.

Greyson Monroe joined the Marines as a young man with a broken heart. Years later he's a wounded warrior trying to reconnect with his spirited daughter and open a ranch for troubled teens. Silver Creek Ranch gave him a start on his healing and with his own ranch, he hopes to complete the journey. The last person he expects to see on his doorstep is Lily Belmont, his college sweetheart turned pop sensation, LaLa Fair.

Lily spent years touring as LaLa Fair living her dream while trying to outrun the heartbreak that life and Greyson Monroe dealt her. When life knocks her down again she crawls out of the spotlight and puts her college degree to good use as a music therapist. Unfortunately for her, life isn't finished kicking her and puts her face-to-face with the man that broke her heart.

Greyson and Lily's unexpected reunion stirs up long-buried feelings and unresolved pain. Will they reignite the love they once shared and work together for the good of the ranch or are the scars of their past too deep to heal?

ISBN: 979-8-9879262-9-1 Paperback

LifeSlice Media

For more information about the author and upcoming works, visit https://terreececlarke.com.

PRAISE FOR HEARTBEAT

"A beautifully written story full of heart, suspense, and love.

J. L. SEEGARS, AUTHOR OF RESTORE ME

"To say this sweeping story is amazing would be an understatement."

CLORRAINE KIBLER, GOODREADS.COM

I was NOT ready❣❣ This book [was] everything, gave what it was supposed to have given, left nothing on the table, it was full full after it ate.

CHRISS MOUNTAIN, GOODREADS.COM

It is so rare to find a new author that can "hit it out of the park" on their first go, but Ms. Clarke has done it.

GDOTZ, AMAZON.COM REVIEW

PRAISE FOR CHASER

"This story had twists and turns I never could have predicted, and during all of that is a beautiful love story between two broken souls that are in need of healing."

EVELYN SOLA, BESTSELLING AUTHOR |
FRIEND ZONED, DOWNFALL AND CRAVE

"Chaser has it all, passion, intrigue and a page turning plot.

KENYA GOREE-BELL, BESTSELLING |
AUTHOR BAD GUY & EASY LIKE SUNDAY
MORNING: THE BLOOD LEGACY SERIES

*Dedicated to songbirds who lose their voices
and fight to find them again.*

"I can be changed by what happens to me. But I refuse to be reduced by it."

MAYA ANGELOU

AUTHOR'S NOTE +
TRIGGER/CONTENT WARNING

Hey reader,

TW/CW things to note - instances or discussion of war, family loss.

Also, there are dialect and grammar choices that are intentional and specific to the regions and cultures highlighted.

If you believe you've found an editing error, first yell your favorite expletive, then shoot the team an email where I too will yell my favorite expletive - hint it begins with an 'f.' Then I shall fix it while raging. It's cathartic. [sbrent@lifeslicemedia.com]

PLAYLIST

Love Me Anyway | (feat. Chris Stapleton) P!nk
Can't Let Go | Anthony Hamilton
Take My Heart | Birdy
Million Reasons | Lady Gaga
California King Bed | Rihanna
Conversations in the Dark | John Legend
Unsteady | X Ambassadors
Iris (Apple Music Home Session) | Josh Ross
BLACKBIIRD | Beyoncé, Tanner Adell, Brittney Spencer,
Tiera Kennedy & Reyna Roberts

Download the playlist on
Apple Music : https://apple.co/4fd8sWA
Spotify:https://spoti.fi/48ebLul

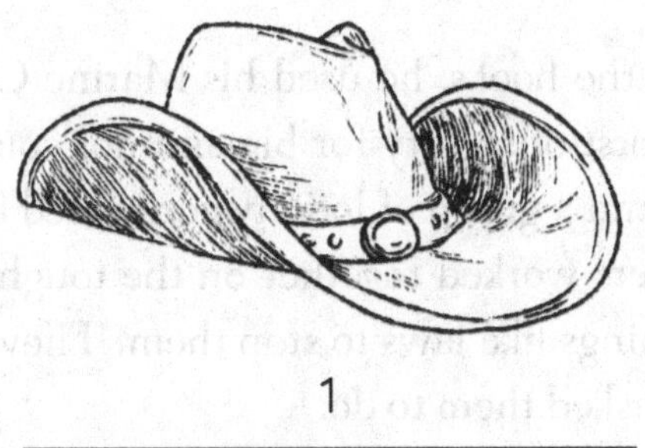

1

WAITING ON PERFECT

GREYSON

"I TOLD YOU I'D CALL WHEN I HAD ANYTHING NEW," THE deep baritone rumbled through the speakers of Greyson's truck.

"That's not the only reason I'm calling. I want to talk about the wildfire projections for the rest of this summer and fall. I've got our first group of kids coming and I need to know if there's going to be trouble. Last thing I want is for these kids to be traumatized more at a place it's supposed to be safe. I know you're focused on what's happening in Colorado and Montana, but I've got a feeling things may get dicey here."

Logan sighed deeply. "You're right to worry. My projections are giving your area a fifty-fifty chance something will break out soon. It's been a long, dry summer Grey. You and your team have prepared well, but at the first sign of trouble, you bug out, hear?"

On paper, Logan Kahale was a search and rescue

specialist. Off the books, he used his Marine Corps training to hunt the worst of society for big and not completely legal bounties. He and a group of loosely connected former armed services brothers worked together on the toughest cases and didn't allow things like laws to stop them. They were perfect for the job he asked them to do.

"I got you. I'm starting to think I should've headed back East to start this program."

"You want to stay near Silver Creek. That's the place that brought you back to civilian life, your touchstone... and after what you've been through you've got to do what's best for you, otherwise you're no good to those kids that are coming to Crystal Fountain to change their lives."

Greyson took in a deep breath and nodded to himself. "Miss Bee always says, 'If you're waiting on perfect, you're going to be waiting a long time.'"

"She ain't wrong," Logan replied with a small chuckle. "Though her cookies are damn near perfection. I could go for a warm chocolate chip one right now."

They chuckled together over Miss Bee's delectable baked goods for a moment before Logan let out a sigh and Greyson tensed in anticipation.

"Listen Grey, I know Ivy is asking a lot of questions about her mom, but are you sure you want to lay this on her right now? LaLa Fair's been spotted in locales across Europe, but my sources tell me she's actually here in the States, lying low. The record company thinks she quit for good. Her publicist hasn't seen her since she left the hospital months ago. They're all worried she's lost it, which tells me she ain't in a good place to be introduced to your little girl."

"It might sound crazy, but this is the perfect time to show Ivy who her mother really is," Greyson growled as he turned onto the road that led to his ranch, Crystal Fountain. "Ivy has built her mother up in her imagination and despite my warnings and Mom's downright demonizing, Ivy is sure she's a misunderstood supermom just waiting for the opportunity to love her. The best way for Ivy to face reality is to have it right in front of her - the mess that is LaLa Fair."

"Shit man, that's a rough way for a kid to meet their parent. To find out she's this famous pop star and that she's a hot fucking mess all in one go?"

"It's the best way to protect her. It's better than her going off on her own when she's eighteen and being sucked into whatever fucked up shit LaLa is doing by then."

"Although..."

"What?"

"It's been ten years, Grey. People change. And there are a lot of inconsistencies in the stories surrounding LaLa. It's hard to pin down which are real, and which were created to generate press."

Greyson threw himself into a parking spot near the front of the restaurant but left the handicap space open for someone with greater needs. Pinching his nose against a hunger, anxiety, and stress induced headache, he tried to will away the memories flashing through his mind...

Lily singing in a darkened nightclub in New York, her eyes glued on him, her lush hips swaying, a secret smile playing on her lips... Lily, dark hair and skin lit by the glow of a small desk lamp as she studied for class, her nose wrinkled in concentration... Lily dancing effortlessly, her belly swollen with their baby girl as she played him her first demo. The empty hospital room...Months of silence before "LaLa Fair's" voice smacked him in the face one day on the way to one of hundreds of doc appointments for Ivy.

"Orgies, drug fueled performances, disappearances attributed to rehab... And now the crash and the hush hush mystery behind it... No. LaLa changed the day she had Ivy. I won't let her destroy Ivy's life like she's destroyed her own, like she almost destroyed mine."

2

MAYBE

LILY

"SING ME TO SLEEP LILY, ONE LAST TIME..."

"Don't say that...Mari! Don't say goodbye...PLEASE!"

"Auntie, wake up!" Her nephew Caleb's rough voice cracked, revealing the adolescence underneath the manly image he had been trying to portray lately. She startled out of the same dream she'd been having for months.

Could you call it a dream when she really was reliving memories? A hellish reality that followed you into sleep, ensuring you could never rest.

She'd slipped up. Since the accident Caleb had been trying to assert himself as man of the house and Lily was trying to assert herself as his new guardian and force him to hold on to what was left of his childhood for as long as he could. They were both failing. Maybe they were both unqualified - he was too young and she was too...her.

Funtime Auntie Lily was the one who always fell asleep when the car started moving because Marigold or someone from her team would take care of the important things. Responsible guardian Lily should have known better than to fall asleep in an Uber in the middle of South Dakota as a single woman with a thirteen-year-old keeping watch.

"You were having another nightmare," he accused.

Sighing, she gripped his hand, now bigger than hers. "Sorry Boogie Bear, I didn't mean to fall asleep."

"Stop calling me that," he grumbled as he pulled away from her hold and got out of the car.

He was so quick to anger, and she didn't blame him. Marigold's death was a blow neither one of them had quite come to grips with yet. He'd lost his mother, she'd lost her sister and now they both were drifting, tossed about in the shit storm that followed the accident. This move was her attempt at finding a safe harbor for them both.

Lily carefully climbed out the back of the car, ignoring the cane beside her, and took in land that stretched out as far as the eye could see with a big, open blue sky stretched over the top. It was beautiful, peaceful, and as far away from the concert stages and paparazzi as she could manage.

"Can I have my phone back?"

"No, Boog—Caleb, you can't. We've already discussed this. You need some time off from the phone, from social media and everything..."

Including those jerks you call friends.

"This ain't fair, Mom would've—"

"Caleb Belmont, the only reason you were allowed to have a phone in the first place is because I advocated for you. Leave it to Marigold and you would've had a flip phone from '95." She leveled a semi-stern look over her glasses at him before she winked.

"You just wanted someone to play Tetris with," he

grumbled with a slight smile. "We don't even do that anymore..."

"I—" Before she could muster up some words of comfort or even luxuriate in the first piece of a smile she'd seen in weeks from Caleb, a tall, thin woman about twenty years her senior wrapped her up in a tight hug and started speaking a mile a minute as she bounced on her toes.

"Howdy! You must be Dr. Belmont! I'm so excited to welcome you to Crystal Fountain Ranch! I still can't believe my luck in landing you. Not to scare you away, but none of the candidates with *half* your experience would take the job for such a small salary, but I threw a *silver dollar* into the fountain and the next day BOOM! Your resume landed in my inbox! I told the boss, you're gonna have to up the salary if you want quality, but he just said to 'figure it out.' And I thought, well Raina if you don't you might as well brush up *your* resume because he's going to throw you out on your rear end. You must be Caleb! Boy, what a handsome one you are! I hear you're a talented musician yourself. Well, you'll have plenty of time to practice around here because after your schoolin' and chores, there's nothing left to do out here but shoot skeet, swim in the lake at your own risk, or watch the clouds go by."

Lily waited for Raina to run out of breath and her ponytail to stop swinging before she spoke. It took a minute. The woman was all kinetic energy. "Thank you for having me. This is a great opportunity to step back into practice full time. Looks like this was perfect for the both of us."

"What fountain?" Caleb asked as he looked around.

"Crystal Fountain. It's up the road a bit, past all the stables and your cottage, but before you get to the gazebo. Legend has it, if you throw in a coin and your heart's desire is pure, your wish will come true. I fought to keep the boss from tearing it down. It's a little wonky, and the water doesn't always spray right, but it's beautiful and has been here since the original owner made their homestead here."

Caleb's eyes showed a keen interest she hadn't seen out of him since the accident. A hint of a smile and a bit of curiosity, all in the first five minutes of arriving. Maybe this really was a good idea. Maybe she really was getting the hang of being Guardian Auntie. Maybe...

* * *

THIS WAS, in fact, not a good idea.

Lily's back was stiff, her leg ached, and her patience was thin. The quaint cottage that came as part of the job package hadn't been cleaned since the mid-nineties at least. Caleb complained about everything from the dirt to the lack of Wi-Fi signal to the boredom. It had been six hours since they arrived, and they were both exhausted and sniping at each other - something they'd never done before. Usually, he tested her sister's patience, and she would break the tension with a laugh, game, or compromise.

Was she supposed to play both roles? No, that wouldn't work. She'd have to be the disciplinarian first. Fun second. Shit, that seemed boring as hell. How did Marigold do this?

"I'm—"

"Bored. Got it, Caleb. You've been bored for the last six hours. Give me a break, shit. I don't know how to make this more entertaining for you, but I wish you'd realize no one thinks cleaning for hours is fun. Though it would take less time if you took the same energy you put into complaining into those baseboards."

Caleb looked stricken, and she immediately felt like shit. "Listen Boogie—"

"I was going to say I was hungry," he mumbled, his eyes on the floor as his chest heaved.

"Shit. Food. Right."

Marigold always made sure Caleb ate on a regular schedule no matter where they were in the world. And here she couldn't even remember that. She wiped her hands on her jeans before she leaned in and put her hands on his shoulders. "I'm sorry Caleb, I shouldn't have snapped. This is a big change for you, and I need to be more mindful of that. Why don't I see which restaurants are close and order something to go, and you go out and explore the ranch. Just don't go too far and keep an eye for anything that might eat you."

"Wait... is that... is that a thing?"

"It's a ranch in the middle of South Dakota," she shrugged. "I'm making an educated assumption."

"Right..." Caleb looked around for a second, snatched up the cane she never used and threw it over his shoulder baseball bat style. He gave her a half-hearted wave and walked out, letting the porch screen slam behind him.

Lily watched him go, a pain in her heart and recrimination in her spirit. His long, lanky build hinted at the man he was becoming. His bowed shoulders revealed the weight of everything he carried. Sighing, she admonished herself one more time before plopping her behind on the couch. Dust plumes rose around her, sending her into a coughing fit as she searched for a local restaurant that delivered. Her asshole physical therapists would be pissed seeing her sit on the low couch, her leg not elevated, but she had a month to get their smaller, sadder family settled and even if she had to limp for the rest of her life, she'd make this a perfect home for Caleb.

"We are going to eat a good meal, finish getting this house ready for the furniture delivery and everything is going to be okay," she told herself as she refastened her scarf around her curls and held back tears. "Nothing else is going to go wrong."

3

LALA

GREYSON

"Shit, how could I forget the music therapist arrived today?" Greyson muttered on his way back to his pickup truck.

He carried his to go order and a delivery order for the ranch. The customer was an L something. The grease smeared receipt was almost impossible to read in some parts, but the address was the cottage he threw in to sweeten the deal for Raina to find a qualified therapist. It looked like she planned on not cooking for the foreseeable future and his shoulder protested the weight of the order and the awkward way he had to carry it. He hoped this meant she was focused on work, that was a great quality in a professional.

The first crew of kids were due to arrive in a month and they just barely gotten everything ready in time. This therapist was the last piece of the team that would make Crystal Fountain Ranch a haven for kids recovering from trauma. If only he could focus on the task at hand... his mind, instead, was consumed by his promise to Ivy that involved a woman who still haunted his dreams. His nightmares, actually.

Gripping the steering wheel tight before releasing it along with a long, slow breath, Greyson reset himself.

"Ivy and the ranch. Those are your priorities," he reminded himself. "Logan will find LaLa and you've prepared all you can to support Ivy and after, LaLa will be a non-issue."

* * *

THE YOUNG TEEN caught Greyson's attention as he drove up the road to the cottage. With his tall and thin frame, he possessed the gangly arms and legs of someone who had recently experienced a growth spurt. He had his dark locs banded up away from his face, wore headphones, a Prince shirt, and hummed a tune while he poked at something on the ground with a cane. Greyson gently tooted the horn to get his attention and waved when he looked up.

"Hey there! You're not the new music therapist, are you?" he joked.

The kid crooked up a half smile that felt familiar before movement at his feet caused him to jump six feet in the air.

"Rattlesnake!"

Before Greyson could put his truck in park, the kid leapt onto the hood.

"Just stay there," Greyson ordered as he rolled down the window all the way and looked more closely at the reptile that wound its way around the teen's discarded headphones on the ground, hissing his irritation at being disturbed. "That's a bull snake. It's not dangerous."

"It doesn't sound not dangerous."

Greyson chuckled. "Fair point. See his markings? They are similar to a rattlesnake, and he puts on a show with all that fussin' and tail shakin', but he's missing a rattle."

"He's a good actor because those fangs look sharp."

"Oh, they are. It'll hurt to get bit, but it's not poisonous." He leaned in to share the snake's secret. Caleb mirrored his movement. "They like to pretend they're rattlers, so predators have the same reaction you did and leave them alone." Greyson pulled out his phone and brought up a photo of a Prairie rattler, reaching it out the window and pointing out the differences to the kid. He appeared to relax a bit but was no closer to getting off the hood of Greyson's truck or reclaiming his headphones on the ground.

Climbing out on his uninjured leg, Greyson slowly moved to the bull snake as the kid sucked in a breath and gave a low 'uh un' behind him. Greyson waited until he was close before grabbing the hissing snake from the back of its head.

"WHOA!" the young man yelped from his station on the hood.

The Bull snake twisted with indignation while Greyson picked up the headphones. Once he had them secured, he let the snake go, and it shot off toward the rocks. He picked up the cane and moved back over to the kid. "Greyson Monroe. I own Crystal Fountain Ranch." He stuck out his hand for a shake.

"Caleb Bel-" he cleared his throat. "Jackson. Caleb Jackson."

The kid gripped his hand firm and looked him in the eye. Greyson liked him already.

"Do you need this to get down?" Greyson moved the cane closer.

"Nah, it's my auntie's. She won't use it, so I took it in case I came across something that could eat me."

Greyson couldn't help but laugh. "I'm on my way to meet your aunt now. Want a ride? I've got your dinner from the diner."

The kid hesitated, and Grey understood. "Or let me park the truck out of the way and I'll walk up with ya. I could use the exercise."

Soon they were matching each other's stride. Their slow amble let him concentrate less on his balance and more on the young man next to him.

"You own all this and do Uber Eats?"

Greyson laughed big again, switching his hold on the food and shrugging off Caleb's nonverbal offer to help. "I was picking up my supper, and they told me they had another order for the ranch. Figured I'd get it here while it's hot. *And it was a chance to meet you and your aunt. Is she a bit stubborn? Is that why she won't use the cane?"

"No, I think she's trying not to show weak-," Caleb shook his head slightly and stood up a little straighter and looked stiffly ahead. "I'm sorry. I don't feel comfortable sharing my aunt's private information."

The sudden change in Caleb's demeanor and tone took Greyson by surprise. He went from regular kid to someone who sounded like he had media training. The response piqued his curiosity, but his counseling training kicked in and he instead sought to show Caleb he respected his boundaries.

"I'm sorry Caleb, I wasn't trying to pry. I was only asking from experience. I refused to use my cane until not using it caught up with me. I was stubborn as a mule, but had to get out of my way for my own healin'. You're right, your aunt's privacy is her own and I'm her employer. I'm sorry for asking an inappropriate question. Thank you for sharing your boundaries."

Caleb gave him a long look with a bit of a side eye like he expected pushback or an angle and when Greyson offered him none, he relaxed a bit and nodded. "You sound like my mom."

"Will she be joinin' you and your aunt soon? I'm sorry I'm clomping in like a big oaf who hasn't done his homework. My assistant found your aunt and put in all the work. There's a lot to get ready before our first set of visitors arrive."

"Mom died a couple months ago."

Greyson's heart broke for the kid. His entire demeanor shifted, and he seemed to shrink into himself.

"That's a rough road man, I'm sorry... How can we support you?"

Caleb shrugged.

"Well, if you need anything. Anything at all, even if it's to talk, I'm a good listener. And if not me, we've got a couple of animals that are better than any licensed human."

That made him smile.

"I'm serious. This whole place is dedicated to healin'," he gestured with a nod to the land off to his left. "Sometimes the goats will whip out their little glasses and notepad when I'm having a tough day, and I tell them all my problems."

Caleb laughed wholeheartedly at his antics. It transformed his face, and Greyson got another strange feeling of familiarity. The kid was still laughing as Greyson described the problems with having goats as therapists.

"That laugh is music to my ears, Boogie Bear. What's so funny?" a quiet, slightly hoarse voice said from behind the screened-in front door.

His heart knew it before his brain could catch up. It beat in triple time and threatened to gallop out of his chest when the door creaked open.

Expecting to see platinum blonde, wavy hair against deep mahogany skin, fluffy obsidian curls tied up in and overflowing the top of a purple satin scarf threw him off. Her signature sunglasses, ones she's worn for every performance and interview, were gone and in their place were simply those eyes. Eyes that in his weak moments he raged against and in his even weaker moments, dreamt about. Those eyes, make up free and widened in shock, mirrored the same eyes that were also his peace - his daughter Ivy's eyes.

Lily swallowed hard, twice, and stepped forward, a slight rock to her step as she went. His eyes dropped to her legs as she moved and she halted, shifting her weight and standing taller. She lifted her nose and peered down at him from her position on the porch.

Shock and something else quickly shifted to something darker and Greyson's heart hardened. A rage he thought he'd worked out and buried on the arid battlefields of Afghanistan and fields of Silver Creek Ranch resurfaced at this, his symbol of triumph and healing - Crystal Fountain Ranch. It shook him to his core, and he felt himself reverting to the cruel and angry man he'd been for far too long. Just as that old demon threatened to unleash, Caleb spoke.

"Auntie Lily, this is Mr. Greyson Monroe, Mr. Greyson. This is my auntie—"

"Dr. Lily Belmont."

"LaLa Fair."

4

____

TOO CLOSE

Lily

IT HAD BEEN TEN YEARS SINCE SHE HEARD HER NAME ON Greyson Monroe's lips and when he finally said it, he used her stage name.

Dick.

The flash of venom in his eyes first chilled then angered her as flashes of his vile behavior ten years ago super-heated her blood. It was his lucky day because she refused to subject Caleb to an ugly scene, but in her mind? In her mind, she was stomping on his balls in glee.

Pull it together Lily. Caleb is watching.

"Thank you for delivering our food, Mr. Monroe. I've already added your tip to the app. Caleb, honey, please take our food in the house."

"You know who she is?! I swear Auntie, I didn't tell him."

She broke eye contact with the slimiest bastard on the planet and gave the best smile she could muster to her nephew. "I knew Mr. Monroe many years ago. You were just a little Boogie Bear then. And look, a decade later and several states away, he's our delivery boy. Life is funny."

Greyson's dark eyes narrowed further and his square jaw ticked at her jab. Caleb cleared his throat and Greyson seemed to remember himself, turning his attention toward her nephew.

"Well, I'll be...Lil Boogie Bear ain't so little anymore," Grey said as he smiled down at her nephew from his six feet four inches. "Now I know why that smile felt so familiar. My God kid, what a handsome, intelligent young man you've grown up to be! The last time I saw you, you were the cutest toddler with the roundest cheeks. I don't suppose you still drop everything to dance when music comes on?"

"Nah," Caleb said, scratching the back of his neck in bashful embarrassment. "I make music now."

Enough of this. Every moment they spent in Greyson's presence made her teeth itch and she wouldn't be able to hold to the niceties much longer.

"Yes, time passes, children grow, circle of life, you probably have to go," she rushed out as she reached out for their food, eager to dismiss the bastard.

She made a mental note to never order from that restaurant while they were in South Dakota, while also trying to remember the terms of her contract with the ranch so she could quickly and with as much grace as she could summon, get out of it.

If Greyson Monroe was in South Dakota, that meant even the entire state of *North* Dakota was too close. Shit, anything west of the Mississippi was now off limits.

She hated to move Caleb again, but there was no fucking way she could stay here with Greyson here, and he obviously still hated her... He'd out her identity in a heartbeat and the fucking circus of paparazzi would descend, the questions would start again, and she would not put Caleb through that.

She was so distracted by the tatters of her life overlapping she missed the maxed out cues her body was giving her. She'd almost reached the bottom of the steps when she misjudged the distance of the next step, and her injured leg took too long to catch up with her momentum. She reached out, but missed the railing, so instead of catching herself, she grabbed only air.

Well, shit on me.

5
____

MEGABITCH

GREYSON

She began her descent like a queen on high, in a pauper's wardrobe of well broken in jeans and a crop top that showed off a nice curve of smooth, grab-able, brown skin and somehow ended up in his arms as warm gravy pooled in his lap.

Typical.

She'd left him with a mess before. At least this time it was gravy and not a sick baby and a broken heart.

Disoriented, she stared up at him with those damn beautiful brown eyes and as she focused; they narrowed and fuck him if she didn't growl at him like some feral cat.

"Auntie, are you ok? Did you hit your head? They said you can't hit your head? DID YOU HIT YOUR HEAD?!"

As soon as she heard the panic rising in his voice, her focus shifted to immediately trying to soothe Caleb while he continued to spiral.

"Boogie Bear, I just missed the step, I'm ok baby," she

said as shrugged herself out of his arms with more force than needed sending him back on his ass as his own leg gave way. Now warm mashed potatoes were sticking to his butt.

"PLEASE BE OK, PLEASE, PLEASE, PLEASE BE OK." Caleb shook his hand as he stared at her unseeing.

"Bear," she whispered as she limped quickly to him and took his face in her hands. "Bear, look at me. I'm fine. CALEB!"

Caleb finally connected, locking eyes with her.

"I'm fine honey, see? I didn't hit my head. I'm perfectly fine. Right here with you," she nodded to him, never breaking eye contact. "I'm here. I'm okay. Okay?"

Caleb started nodding with her. "Okay. You're okay." He sniffed long before his face cracked and tears of relief flooded his eyes and overflowed down his cheeks.

"Oh Boogie..." she cooed, bringing him tight to her and hugging him as he continued to break down.

Once he was sure they were stable, Greyson looked at the mess of dinner on the ground and busied himself with cleaning it up. Caleb didn't need an audience for this tough moment. He made his way to the kitchen of the cottage, salvaging what he could until they both came in, eyes red and looking exhausted.

"I was able to save some of the food," he said as he finished plating the food for the two of them. Caleb avoided his eyes as he mumbled a thanks and took a plate from his outstretched hands. He kissed his aunt on the cheek before he shuffled off to one of the bedrooms off the living room.

LaLa watched him as he went, her lip trembling. Once he closed the door, she wiped away the wet from her eyes and took a couple deep breaths, tapping her hand against her thigh as she breathed.

Feelings he didn't want to feel surfaced as he watched her, a protectiveness over her and Caleb and profound sadness for all of them. Anger was a more familiar beast, in some ways a safer one. Still, Lily was a human being, and she was hurtin'.

"I'm sorry to hear about Marigold. I knew about the accident, but not who died. She was a good woman and judging by Bryson, I mean Caleb, continued to be a phenomenal mom," he said and he meant it. LaLa and her sister were inseparable when he met both of them in college. LaLa spent practically every weekend in Marigold's dorm until she graduated from NYU and joined them as an official grad student.

When Marigold fell pregnant, it was LaLa who moved them into an apartment and started singing in nightclubs to support Mari and baby Caleb, then called Bryson, when the professor that had gotten Mari pregnant went back to his wife. Before she was LaLa, she was Lily, a woman who loved kids and was quick to toss him the diaper bag and snag Caleb's car seat, turning their dates into a moment of rest for Mari.

Shaking off the memories, he grabbed the second plate, set it on the half counter separating the great room from the kitchen, and moved to stride past her. His heart stopped, then painfully kicked over again when she reached out and touched his arm. He moved slightly out of her reach.

LaLa pursed her lips and crossed her arms, withdrawing into herself. "I had a concussion from the accident. They were worried about a secondary concussion. That's why... Anyway, not for me, I know you wouldn't do shit for me, but for Caleb, please don't tell anyone we are here. The pressure of LaLa Fair is too much and no kid should have to live in that after what he's been through. He needs to heal. We only use his middle name and mom's maiden name to keep him safe, to let him have a good life...So.."

Her reaching for him created a longing that he hated, and he barked a little. "I have no interest in bringing the LaLa Fair Circus to my ranch."

"Your–"

He crossed his arms in satisfaction as understanding, then horror bloomed across her face.

"Yes, LaLa, I'm your boss."

"I quit."

* * *

Lily

She must've been a mega bitch in another life because the level of bullshit splattering against the windowpane of her current life was more than should be allowed.

Lily flipped through messages from her body double in Europe, LaTavia.

Ms. LaLa, thank you so much for this wonderful opportunity to travel the world and dedicate myself to my studies. I am ready for the bar and after I am starting a new job in housing legal aid. You have made it possible for me to see the most amazing things and live an extraordinary life, but I'm ready to be me now and I can afford to use my degree to really help people. Because of you, I'm debt free and have a nest egg. That means I can do this important work for years. I can honor my mom and work to make sure that families don't experience homelessness like we did because they didn't have access to people who could help them. I wish you'd let me out of the NDA so I could tell the world about the REAL you.

-LaTavia

Just what she needed. Resisting the urge to throw her phone, she fired off an appropriately kind response. She really liked LaTavia and was happy for her, but selfishly she just didn't want to deal with one more issue. And she really didn't want to put LaLa Fair back in rehab.

"I tithe, I donate to a host of do gooding organizations, I've tried to be a good person in this life so what the fuck God?" she asked as she limped back and forth in front of Crystal Fountain. She tipped her head back and looked up to the heavens, even though she didn't expect a response.

"Perhaps it's the 'what the fuck part' in the same sentence as His name," a deep voice rumbled behind her.

For the second time in one day, she almost fell on her ass. She caught herself in time and hid her cane behind her back. Better this stranger thought she was clumsy rather than a hobbled target.

After Greyson's smug declaration, she promptly quit and kicked him out of the cottage. Then she placed several, increasingly frantic, phone calls to her lawyers. At some point, she left the house so Caleb wouldn't overhear and ended up here at the fountain. She should have been more responsible than to be out walking the property this late.

"I didn't mean to scare you, Ms. Fair. I'm here on behalf of Greyson."

"So much for no interest in the circus," she grumbled, mentally calculating how quickly the press could descend on this place. "How much does he want? Or does he want me to counter a tabloid offer?"

The tall, powerfully built man put up his hands in a

gesture of submissive peace and stepped closer so that the lights around the fountain caught his objectively handsome face. He smiled, showing off a prominent eye tooth that gave him a wolfish appearance, but something about his smile made her take a second, then a third step back.

"I'm Logan Kahale and I mean you no harm..."

There was an unspoken "yet" they both heard loud and clear. That earned two more steps back and her cane brought to the front.

"I'm here to find out your intentions toward the Monroe family."

Lily kept her posture straighter than the pain radiating through her leg up to her hip should've allowed and spoke with a bravery she certainly didn't feel. She raised her voice above the soft, damn near whisper speak she'd adopted to save what was left of her voice. She had the distinct feeling the voice she used tonight would either save or end her life.

"I have no intentions of anything toward that family. If I never come across them again, I'd be too glad. I came here to get my nephew away from LaLa Fair's life. I've got shit luck lately, and it keeps getting worse. Greyson isn't listed on any of the company's information and supposedly the foundation funding this place has a great reputation. Obviously, I was mistaken. There is not a single reason for me to ever cross paths with Greyson Monroe, and I certainly wouldn't seek him out and drag my nephew along. Greyson told me exactly where to go ten years ago."

Something flashed in the man's face, but it was gone before she could figure it out. Maybe he was trying to decide where to put her body. A man like him struck her as someone who had plenty of places to hide them.

"Ms. Fair, what about your daughter?"

Ivy.

No one ever talked about Ivy. Lily would've preferred if he'd just punched her in the face instead. She rubbed the spot on her chest where the pain sat, too deep to ever really soothe.

"No one ever asks me about her," she whispered. "It makes sense...the number of people alive who know about Ivy can be counted on one hand. Mari and our mother are gone. The midwife who delivered Ivy retired and shit, Greyson and his mother made it clear they blamed me."

She gave up on being brave and sank onto the edge of the fountain. If this man was going to do her harm, he would do it. She set the cane next to her and began spinning the ring on her right ring finger around. "I grieved so hard those first few birthdays they thought about involuntarily admitting me... Eventually, I learned to hide the pain. Existing in this dance where the broken pieces of your heart are too painful for everyone else, so you brutalize yourself in silence to keep everyone else ok. Is that what you wanted to know? How I've suffered for ten years? How I'll never be okay until the day I see her again? Is that enough for your employer?"

Greyson stormed out of the shadows, dark brown eyes made darker by his apparent rage. "So you do plan on being with her? Was this job your way of circumventing my rights?!"

Her head snapped back at his anger and odd question. "What fucking rights would you have over whether I see Ivy again? I know you've always thought you controlled the sun as it rose and set, but even you don't have control over that, you fucking weirdo."

"Grey, I told you to hang back and let me talk to her."

"Intimidate me, you mean?" Lily shot back at Logan

before turning back to Greyson. "I have as much right to Lily as you do! I did the best I COULD!"

"You gave up all rights ten years ago, LaLa," he growled back.

"STOP BLAMING ME! I TRIED! I did everything I was supposed to do!"

"Everything but stick around, Lily! YOU DID EVERYTHING BUT BE WHAT SHE NEEDED! SHE NEEDED HER MOMMA ALL THOSE DAYS IN THE NICU, ALL THE DAYS SINCE, SHE NEEDED YOU TOO!"

Greyson stormed away along the road, back toward the main house.

She sat weeping on the side of the fountain for several moments as Greyson's footsteps faded into the distance and the venom of his words coursed through her veins, killing her with each heartbeat.

"From now on, I'll be your contact regarding this matter until Grey's lawyers reach out," Logan said.

"This is an at will state and I quit. I'm taking Caleb as far away from here as I can get first thing tomorrow morning."

"You're giving up, just like that? What about all the suffering?"

"What is there to give up? I—" Greyson's words, the actual words, not the venom of them, suddenly hit her. "Days. He said days in the NICU. How long was she in the NICU?"

"I don't see why that—"

"TELL ME! How long did she survive? Mrs. Monroe said she died shortly after she was born, before I woke up, but Greyson said days. Why would he say days in the NICU?"

"He misspoke, Ms. Fair. I'm sorry. Let me walk you back to the cabin."

Lily didn't know what to feel. Grief, her steady companion, mixed with the guilt she had tried to exorcise from her life. Somewhere there was a moment of horror at the thought that she'd gotten the wrong information and missed the chance to say goodbye to her little girl when she left the hospital against medical advice. There was the moment of relief that wasn't the case, then self-recrimination at feeling relief.

She had to get the hell out of this place. Like Greyson, it was deceptive. It looked like a place where you anchor your heart, but once you committed, it delivered blow after blow of pain.

* * *

"GREY, you've got a big fucking problem," Logan said as he glanced at his watch.

"So what she has more money than I do. She signed away her rights ten years ago and did not establish contact with Ivy since. There is not a judge in the state that will side with her. Especially cutting out on a sick baby."

"That's the thing man, I don't think she signed anything. At least not knowingly... You may want to sit down."

"Cut the dramatics, man. What the fuck did she tell you?"

Logan scrubbed his hand down his face, looking all of his forty-plus years. His dark eyes were wary.

"She thinks Ivy died as an infant, because that's what your mother told her."

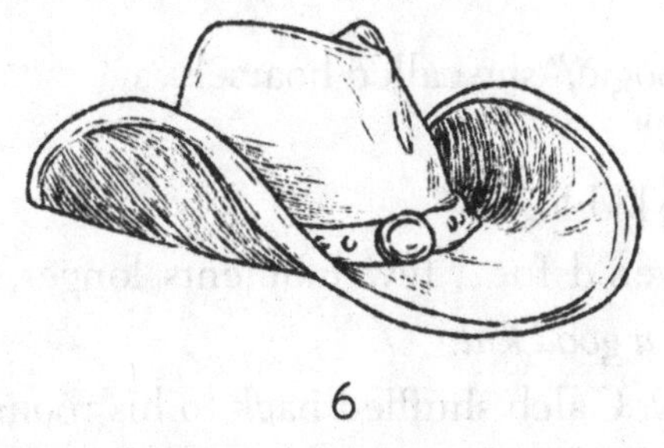

6

BEAUTIFUL AND HEALTHY

GREYSON

Whatever he'd braced for Logan to say, it sure as fuck wasn't that and it took him way too long to process it.

He couldn't remember anything from the moment Logan uttered the sentence that rocked his world until now. It was like he didn't connect with anything other than pain until his eyes settled on her sleeping face. She grimaced as she adjusted on the air mattress that seemed as expensive and fancy as a proper bed.

"Don't say that...Mari! Don't say goodbye...PLEASE! SOMEBODY! HELP US, God help us...Ivy..."

It took everything in him not to go to Lily's side. When she called for their daughter... the reality of the situation crashed down on him again, threatening to break his back in two. Greyson just sat in the chair across from her bed and kept watch over her.

A small knock on the door brought her out of her nightmare.

"I'm ok Boogie," she called hoarsely.

"You sure?"

"I promise kiddo."

Caleb hovered for a few moments longer, listening for his aunt. *Such a good kid.*

Eventually, Caleb shuffled back to his room and Lily let out a slow breath, her hand on her chest. If she saw him now, she'd scream and frighten Caleb. His body wasn't what it used to be, but he was happy he could still move through darkness like a shadow. He had his hand over her mouth before she could react. It was overdramatic, but he felt like sanity had left him hours ago.

"It's me, Grey. I'm not here to hurt you. I have something important to tell you, and I didn't want you to scare Caleb. Okay? Nod twice if you understand."

She dropped her head, and he relaxed his hand. Then the crazy woman head butted him with the back of her head. He saw stars shooting around the dark room and felt the gush of warm, wet fluid that followed.

"You broke my nose Lily!" He whispered yelled. Holding his nose between his hands, he adjusted it back in place with a muffled grunt. While he fixed his nose, she rolled across the air mattress like a pissed off armadillo and hopped, limped across the room.

"Ok, I had that coming," he sighed, digging into his pocket for a kerchief and holding his face over the side of the bed so he wouldn't drip on it. "And I deserve so much more." He got up and headed toward the bathroom. "Don't go anywhere, ok? It's about Ivy."

* * *

LILY

"Don't go anywhere, ok? It's about Ivy."

Well, that froze her right where she stood.

Lily's heart thrummed in her head, making her lightheaded. She had gone from a nightmare, soothing Caleb, to having the strange feeling of being watched, to the horror of discovering someone in her room, and finally, the anger of realizing it was Greyson.

Boy, I miss having a security team.

She thought she'd taken a calculated risk in leaving them to escort her body double, but these two nighttime encounters with very big cowboys (and not in a good way) had her thinking otherwise.

She flipped on the light, breathed in the warm mist of her humidifier, and sucked on a honey drop while she waited for the water in the bathroom to turn off. When he reemerged, she almost felt bad for him. She'd definitely broken his nose. The swelling and bruising bloomed across his face, his light chambray shirt dotted with a good amount of blood.

"You have two minutes."

"This is bigger than two minutes Lily," Grey said as he sat his heavy, muscular self on her bed.

Her mouth pressed in tight - outside clothes on the bed. She hated it. Now wherever Greyson had sat his ass on all day was in her bed. Horses, public chairs...

God, I can't wait to get the hell out of here.

He took off his cowboy hat and stared at it. "Where do you think Ivy is now?"

The question had her spinning her ring again, but the

look on his face? The pain on his face brought back all the guilt.

"If I hadn't insisted on giving birth at home... If she hadn't..." She took a deep breath and looked out the window. "I like to imagine she'd be planning her eleventh birthday party and fighting for the Tetris champion title with Boogie... My faith tells me she's with people that love her like Mari and Mom. And I carry her with me always, here," she pointed to that sore spot in her chest, "and here," Lily held out the ring she never took off. "Mari had jewelry made with her ashes for me, mom and for herself. We never talked about her, not really, but we carried her with us. Always."

"My mother gave you those ashes?"

The anger in his voice cut. Deep. She quickly pulled her hand back to her, protectively covering it with her left hand as he looked like he wanted to rip the ring off of her finger.

"I have every right to her too Greyson," she hated the way her voice shook. "I didn't want to be treated like gum on someone's shoe the way the hospital treated Mari when she had Caleb. At home with a midwife seemed better, healthier for both of us. I'll carry that guilt for the rest of my life, no matter how many hours of therapy I endure. But I've learned enough to know I don't deserve your scorn. I didn't then and I don't now. And your two minutes are up."

She moved to leave when suddenly he was at her back, his hand pressing the door closed.

"Please...Lily..."

Moisture dripped on her shoulder and tank. She whipped around. "Your blood is—"

He was crying. It was the second time she'd seen him cry. The first was when he learned his father died while they were in grad school.

"I'm so sorry Lily. I fucked up. I fucked up so bad. I– she–, Jesus Lily," he took a deep breath and blew it out. "Ivy is alive. Our baby girl is alive, beautiful, and healthy. I didn't know you thought...She lied to us... I'm so...sorry."

He searched her eyes and waited and she? Well, she LOST. HER. SHIT.

* * *

GREYSON

"Ivy?" she whispered in disbelief. "Ivy's alive?"

"Yes, she's–"

"Who took her? How did you find her? HOW–"

He took a chance she wouldn't clock him and placed his hands on her arms to brace her and move her to the bed, helping her sit. "She wasn't kidnapped. I've raised her best as I could with mom's help. She'll be home from boarding school in a month and–"

"I'm sorry. I think I'm having delusions. WHAT did you say?"

"Auntie?"

"You knew my daughter was alive for TEN YEARS and you never told me? You let me believe, *grieve* for a decade–"

Caleb slipped the door open, his eyes wide as he took in the both of them. He lingered on Grey's broken nose. "Mr. Monroe, I'm gonna have to ask you to leave."

Dammit. This was turning to shit.

"I appreciate you takin' up for your aunt Caleb, but we're working through something and.."

Lily stood and paced damn near hyperventilating until suddenly she picked up her suitcase near the window and threw it. The big bay window cracked. She picked the suitcase up again and threw it again.

"MY BABY!"

Chink! The window splintered more.

"MY BABY!"

Chink! Chink! Spiderwebs of crack ricocheted as the glass shook under the force of Lily's assault.

"ALL THIS TIME!

CRASH!

The window shattered and so did she, falling to her knees in tears and rage.

"WHOSE ASHES AM I WEARING? WHO DID I BURY WITH MY *MOTHER*, MY *SISTER*?!"

"I don't know..." he admitted as he sank to the floor next to her.

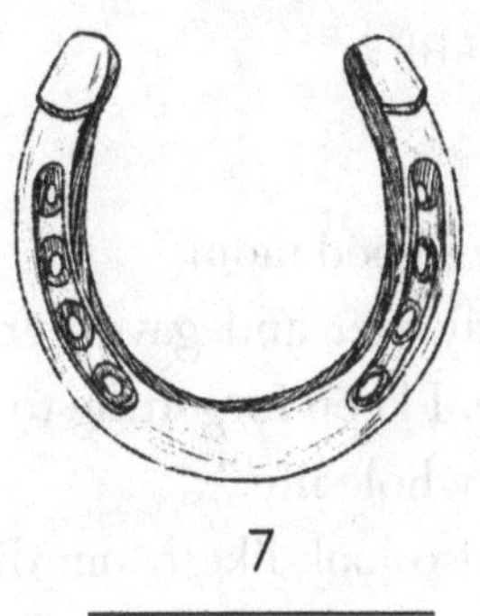

7

SAME SIDE

LILY

"Sounds like Mr. Monroe's mom is a bitch," Caleb said over breakfast later that morning.

Logan arrived as the sun rose with breakfast items and helpfully suggested Greyson leave with him to give her and Caleb time to adjust to the news. They had spent the hours since his confession in teary silence. Why did it feel like they were grieving all over again?

"You shouldn't call women bitches, Boogie," she said gently as she tugged off his hoodie and smoothed his locs. "But...you're not wrong. I just can't believe it...There's still so much I still don't know."

"What do you think she's like?" he asked with a mouth full of bacon.

"We're going to find out, sooner than later," she growled as she tapped a pen.

"Auntie?"

"Yeah, Boog?"

"You're gonna be a good mom."

Lily blinked away wet and gave her nephew a watery grin. "I'm not so sure. I keep forgetting to feed you Boog and I've known you your whole life."

"Yeah, but you also look like Mom did when she found out about those kids stealing my stuff at school and the school didn't believe me. She hulked out and I think, unless Mr. Monroe figures this out real quick, you're gonna Hulk Smash this whole ranch. But you should also stop me from swearing, not just who I aim it at."

"Shit. You're right."

* * *

SHE PEEKED in on Caleb as he took a midmorning nap. He still slept like he did when he was a baby - on his back spread eagle like sleep hit him with an uppercut. She closed his door and considered taking a nap herself, but as soon as the idea appeared in her mind, the little girl she'd only imagined gave her renewed energy...and anger.

Lily stormed as quickly as she could move across the ranch with a single purpose—she wanted her baby.

Every cell in her body felt electric, buzzing with the surge of emotions that had overwhelmed her since they started to piece together the truth. She wasn't sure how she'd made it through the night without losing her mind. The shock, the anger, the gut-wrenching sorrow—it was all too much. It pressed her down and held her in place. That energy had shifted, and she needed to know everything. She wouldn't rest until she had the full truth about Ivy.

She knocked twice before letting her herself into his home uninvited. She figured he wouldn't or couldn't mind, considering he pulled some weirdo stalker shit last night before dropping the nuke that blew up her entire world.

She was halfway through the living room, calling his name before he appeared at the top of the stairs. She skidded to a halt when she saw him. Shirtless, he descended the stairs slowly, his eyes locked on her, but the condition of his torso distracted her. Part of him was completely flawless, smooth skin stretched over muscles much larger than he had ten years ago, the rest was stretched, shiny skin that looked pieced together in spots with seams tracing across his body and disappearing around his back.

"Don't stare."

Her eyes snapped back to his, and his face hardened. She felt bad about the staring and the black eyes and tape across his nose.

"Does it hurt?"

"The nose or the grafts?"

She shrugged. "Either, both, whatever you want to tell me."

"Most of the time the grafts don't anymore... Other times I feel like I'm still on fire."

She didn't realize she had moved toward him until she felt the warmth and texture of his skin beneath her fingers. He stilled on the bottom step. "How?"

"I received a permanent vacation earlier than I planned, courtesy of an IED."

She took in the wry smile on his face, and it struck her as wrong. "You shouldn't joke about that."

"You don't get to decide," he growled and moved past

her, giving her a view of the extent of his scars on his back. They went up the back of his neck and spidered over his otherwise smooth bald head.

"You get your fill Lily?"

"I don't mean to...um...thank you–"

"Don't...Jesus, don't fucking thank me for my service. Just tell me what you need." He shrugged on his snug, long-sleeved shirt over his hard body and sat on the edge of the couch.

She shook herself out of her rudeness and focused on why she was there. "I need to know everything about Ivy. Everything. I'm not leaving until you tell me, so cancel whatever you've got planned today," she demanded, her voice hoarse.

Greyson nodded, his face softening. "I'll clear my schedule," he said quietly, grabbing his phone from his pocket. After a brief conversation with someone on the other end, he hung up and turned to her. "Come with me."

Lily followed him in silence, her heart pounding in her chest as they walked further into his house. She was still trying to wrap her mind around the enormity of it all—the daughter she thought had died, the lies Greyson's mother had spun, and the years of lost time. Through it all, her brain just kept whispering, "Ivy's alive."

Eagerly, she looked around the walls for a glimpse of her baby and was disappointed and worried when she didn't find a single photo.

"Ivy likes to do the decorating whenever we move. She sends the sketches and I follow them to a tee or there's hell to pay," a small smile played on his lips. "She hangs the photos when she comes home. Says she needs to be in person to get the 'vibe' of the place."

Lily's throat felt like it would swell shut. She felt the same way. She never hung photos until she had lived in the space for a while and understood its energy.

Greyson pushed open the door to his study and led her inside. It was quiet, dark and manly with heavy wood furniture and built-ins. The thick rug cushioned their footfalls, and in the quiet, it held a certain reverence.

"Have a seat," he said, pointing to a large leather sofa situated close to the door.

Lily sat down on the edge of the sofa, her hands trembling as she waited. The quiet gurgle of a fountain in the corner was the only sound in the room, each second dragging out longer than the last.

Greyson pulled several volumes of books off the shelf to her left and when his arms were full, he set them down gently on the coffee table and sat across from her, the weight of the past heavy between them.

"These are everything," he said, his voice low. "Every year of her life."

Lily stared at the photo albums, her eyes prickling as the reality of what was in front of her sank in.

Ivy's life, the life she should have known, documented year by year—photographs, milestones, moments she had missed. That spot in her chest ached deeply.

"Why didn't you tell me sooner?" she whispered, her voice cracking.

Greyson's jaw clenched. "I didn't know how. I didn't even know the full extent of what my mother had done until you asked Logan about the NICU. I still don't know if I understand everything. Logan's looking into it now." He rubbed his hands over his bald head in frustration and his eyes pleaded with her to believe him.

"All mom told me was that you said you couldn't deal with a sick baby and your singing career. She said you'd signed over your parental rights and checked out of the hospital room against doctor's orders. By the time I got to *your* hospital, you were gone and Ivy was so sick... I couldn't be by her side and search for you at the same time. I didn't have the resources I have now."

Lily shot him a look, eyes wet with unshed tears. "You didn't know? I called you and you screamed at me. 'How could I be so irresponsible?' 'The time to do the right thing was before this all happened, Lily—'" She stopped, the memories of his coldness and anger cutting into her like shards of glass.

"I was wrong," Greyson said quietly, his voice thick with regret. "I thought you didn't care. That you just signed her away because you didn't want the responsibility. My mother fed me lies, and I believed them. I was grieving, scared, confused... angry. One moment I have the dream - a fiancé and a new baby - and the next moment you both almost died and then you were gone. I had no reason not to believe her."

Lily's eyes filled with tears, her heart aching. She remembered her time in the hospital after she woke up—the exhaustion, the numbness after Mrs. Monroe told her Ivy hadn't made it, and the papers she'd signed in a haze, too broken to even read what they were.

"I thought she was gone," Lily whispered, wiping her eyes roughly. "I thought I lost her that day. She was... your mother was so kind to me. For the first time, she was really actually warm to me. She *cried* with me, said that your behavior horrified her, that you blamed me because I wanted Ivy to be born at home. She said she wanted to be there because mother-to-mother she understood how I felt."

Lily shook her head. "Who just has parental rights waivers on their person? I knew she didn't agree with us having a baby so soon and my wishes, but...to tell me Ivy was dead..."

Greyson's hand twitched, as if he wanted to reach for her, but he stopped himself and hung his head. "She's alive, Lily. And she's been asking about you. For years, she's asked about her mother. I sent Logan to find you. As fate would have it, you were already on your way back to her."

Lily's breath hitched at the words. Ivy had been asking about her? Her heart ached at the thought of her daughter, a stranger to her now, wanting to know who she was. The gravity of what she'd missed, what they'd both missed, weighed heavily on her chest.

Greyson nodded, pushing the first album toward her. "This is from the first year," he said, his voice soft. "She's strong like you are. She fought so hard those first weeks."

Lily's hands trembled as she opened the album. The first page showed a picture of a tiny baby girl with a head full of ebony curls, tubes attached to every part of her. Her tiny fingers curled around a finger, Grey's finger, tight.

"She was beautiful," she whispered, tracing the outline of her daughter's face with her fingertip.

"She still is," Greyson said, his voice thick with emotion. "She's always had your eyes and round little nose."

Lily turned the pages slowly, absorbing each photo—first smiles, first steps, birthdays. Ivy's life unfolded in front of her, and the pain of missing out on every moment crushed her. Each page served as a painful reminder of what she had lost, of all the years she had been denied.

Greyson sat silently across from her, watching as she flipped through the albums, his own emotions raw. "She's strong, just like you," he reiterated softly. "And stubborn too."

Lily let out a shaky laugh, the first sign of lightness she'd felt in hours. "I wonder where she gets that from," she muttered, her voice barely above a whisper.

A knock at the front door took Grey out of the room for a few moments. When he returned, Caleb was with him.

"I wanted to make sure you were ok," Caleb said before he sat close and peered at the most current album. "Wow, she looks a lot like you and Mom in that picture that Grandma kept in the living room."

"Yeah," was all she could get out.

They fell into silence again, the only sound the turning of pages as Lily and Caleb continued to soak in the lost years.

After a while, an alarm on her watch went off. "Feed Caleb" flashed.

"What did that say?" He asked incredulously.

"Nothing," she mumbled.

He picked up her phone with the notification clearly on display. "Auntie. 'Feed Caleb?'"

"You do want to eat, don't you?"

He dropped his head and shook it slightly. "I could also just tell you when I'm hungry. I'm not a little kid anymore."

"Help yourself to anything you find in the kitchen," Grey said, smiling at him.

When Caleb had gone, his face turned more serious. "If it's okay with you, I think she should finish the rest of the school year before she meets you," Greyson said after a moment. "It'll give you time to prepare and for us to work through...everything."

Lily closed the album slowly, her emotions swirling. "I

both don't think I can wait to see her, and don't know how to be her mother, Greyson. I don't know where to start."

He leaned forward, his voice gentle. "Just be honest with her. She's been asking about you for a long time, Lily. So this is a bigger shock for you than her, and maybe taking this time will give you both the reunion you deserve."

Lily swallowed the lump in her throat and looked up at him, her eyes filled with a mixture of fear and hope. "I don't know how to forgive you. Forgive myself for this," she admitted. "But I want to be there for her now."

Greyson nodded, the weight of his own guilt and anger pressing heavily on his shoulders. "I don't expect you to forgive me. I won't forgive me. But I'll help you learn about her. I'll do whatever it takes to make this right."

He started to get up and changed his mind, instead scooting closer to her. His jaw clenched and unclenched, the words he wanted to say catching in his throat.

"I've been angry with you for so long, Lily," he finally said, his voice rough and low. "So damn angry. I blamed you for everything—for walking away, for choosing fame and leaving me and Ivy behind. And now…" He stopped, his eyes locking with hers. "Now, I don't know what to do with it. I don't know how to process any of this."

"I thought you didn't care," he continued, his voice shaking slightly. "And I carried that with me for years. It became a part of me. It ate holes through me."

He moved closer to her, his voice softer now, filled with a vulnerability she barely recognized anymore. "But now… we know some of the truth. And I don't know what to do, Lily. I don't know how to undo all that hurt. But we have a month. A month to figure it out for that beautiful little girl with her momma's eyes. I went to war for her Lily. I went to war to get her the care and security she needed. I never hesitated. And now I can make peace for her to bask in the love she has always deserved and desperately needs. *Your* love."

They sat in silence, the years they'd lost stretching between them like a vast chasm. But for the first time in ten years, Lily felt like they were both standing on the same side.

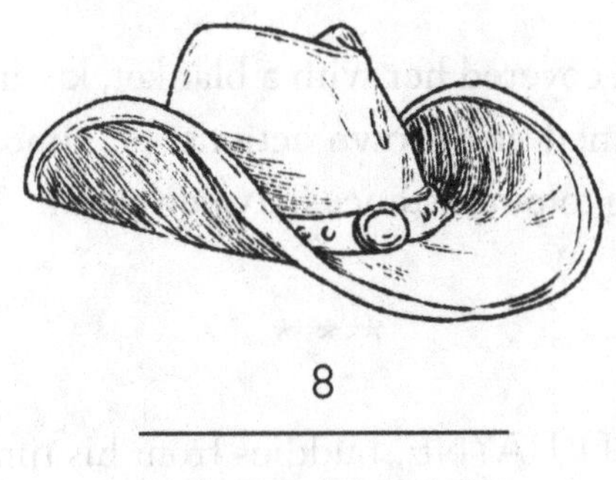

8

NO PROMISES

GREYSON

HE WENT TO SEE ABOUT CALEB AND GIVE LILY SOME space.

If he was being honest, he needed space, too. He needed to get out of this house and put some sweat therapy in and it arrived as a moving truck trundling up the lane toward Lily's cottage. He finished up the quick meal he'd helped Caleb finish making and made a plate for Lily.

Greyson panicked when he saw she'd left the office, but instinct led him to Ivy's room where he found a sleeping Lily curled up in Ivy's bed clutching one of her stuffies, her face still wet. He was dumbstruck as he took in the scene in front of him. She looked so much like Ivy, it almost brought him to his knees. She'd lost so much. There was no way they could navigate this on their own.

Shaking himself out of his stupor, he texted the therapist from Silver Creek and arranged for him to stop by later in the week. Then he took a moment to set the plate on the nightstand and covered her with a blanket, kissing her on the shoulder. Stunned at his own actions, he almost ran out of the room trying to put distance between them.

* * *

DRAVEN AND RAYNE, buddies from his time recovering at Silver Creek Ranch, were putting the final touches on the beds while their women, Cashea and Billie, sorted out bedding.

Raina and her granddaughter went to work in the kitchen, making moves around him and Caleb as they got to the bottom of the slow drains in the kitchen and bathrooms.

"It's no use Boogie. I think we've got to dig up the pipe out back. I bet it's gonna need to be replaced. Ever operate a backhoe before?"

The kid's eyes were wide with excitement, and despite everything going on, Grey couldn't help but smile back.

"Well, whatever you're going to do, do it quick," Raina fussed. "I can't believe you forgot to have this cottage cleaned and aired out. Some way to welcome someone you're paying peanuts of their worth."

"Lily's not a pampered princess," he said with a laugh. "She once shoved her purse in front of Caleb so he could throw up in it."

"Eww, really?" Caleb looked horrified.

"Yep, right in the middle of the Dollar Store. She was buying Christmas presents, and that's when we discovered you were allergic to fruit punch."

"It's the dyes," Caleb muttered, scratching the back of his head as he snuck a glance over at Raina's granddaughter.

"Well, her luxurious sheets say otherwise," Cashea said,

as she came out of the bedroom. "That's a bed fit for a queen. Makes me want to pull a Goldilocks."

The reminder of the difference in her life now slid the smile right off his face. "Yeah, we should... we should get to it."

* * *

LILY

For the first time in months, she had a restful sleep. It was like her brain shut off and she just drifted in darkness for... checking her watch...SIX HOURS?! She sat up so quick she forgot where she was for a moment.

Ivy.

She looked around again at the turquoise and lime room with a wide grin. It was preteen perfection, with its bed full of stuffies and bookcases full of books and awards. Ivy was a smart cookie who loved animals. Lily wouldn't be surprised if she became a veterinarian.

Thoughts of Caleb were the only thing that got her to leave the room. The still house and setting sun that greeted her made her nervous, and she set out to find her Boogie.

"Your chariot awaits, Dr. Belmont," Raina said as she looked up from the book she was reading and waved her over to the very nice golf cart she sat in. "I'm supposed to take you back to your cottage if you're ready."

Lily grinned as she limped over, grateful for the ride. She'd overdone it the last few days and, being without a reliable physical therapist, she felt like she was going backwards on her progress.

"Want to drive? Get used to using it?" Raina offered.

"Oh, I've driven these before on tour—tour of wineries n' such," Lily corrected as she slid onto the driver's seat and Raina scooted over.

"What are you reading?" she asked to further distract Raina from her slip up.

"Rereading Michelle Midnight's series again. She hasn't released new books now in forever. They are my comfort reads."

"I haven't been able to read for pleasure in years. I'll add them to my list."

As she came around the bend, the cottage came into view and she smiled big. The porch was now a cozy oasis with the chairs and all weather rugs she'd selected. Pretty plants in colorful planters offered cheery pops of colors.

"The boss wanted to help you all get settled, especially after you had to spend yesterday cleaning. It was supposed to be ready when you arrived."

"Oh gosh, thank you," she said quietly. She quickly parked the cart and moved inside with Raina pointing out the additions Greyson and his friends had made to the home. Seeing her artwork carefully set against the longest wall, she smiled.

"You gotta feel the vibe first," she whispered to herself.

"We ran into one problem," Raina said, as she rushed ahead of her to the kitchen. "The slow drains are because of tree roots in the drainpipe. Caleb has been quite the helper to Grey. That's one good kid."

"He's the best," Lily agreed as she looked out the window over the sink. "He's not old enough to operate a tractor!"

"That's a backhoe," Raina called out as Lily moved to the backdoor ready to tear Greyson a new one. *She* was Caleb's guardian. He should have asked her permission. Caleb was a child...He was...

"...handling that backhoe like he's been doing it all of his life."

She watched the last twenty minutes of his work, with Grey patiently sitting beside him, every so often pointing things out, but for the most part, he let Caleb work. And her nephew, whose fingers played Chopin and Hendrix with artistry, applied the same depth and focus to John Deere.

By the time they finished, the moon was rising and Raina had brought out the sweetest, freshest lemonade and some simple, but delicious, sandwiches. They sat together eating, chatting, and waiting for the guys to finish.

Soon enough, Caleb and Greyson were climbing down and turning off the industrial lights that illuminated the area. Caleb, eyes alight, grinned from ear to ear.

"Did you see that Auntie? We had to dig to check out the pipe, which was filled with old paint and tree roots. Then we cut it out, replaced it, and Grey let me fill in by myself!"

"I saw Boog. You looked legit out there."

"Ooh, food!"

"Wash up first."

"Wash up first."

Lily and Greyson met eyes after they spoke in unison, stopping Caleb in mid reach.

"But I'm hungry..."

"Then you better hurry, man," Greyson said good-naturedly.

"Here, have a sip," Lily said, holding up her lemonade and straw. Caleb took two long drags, emptying it and cracking his aunt up.

"Oh, that's goood," he said with a smile before galloping off into the house.

"Well, I'm going to get going," Raina said as she slapped her hands against her thighs and stood. "These are yours Doc."

Lily caught the keys to the golf cart. "But–"

"The ranch is a big place. You need to get around safely while you continue to heal," Greyson interrupted her.

"This is as good as it's going to get unless I lose a hundred pounds, according to the last two physical therapists I worked with," Lily said with a shrug.

"What?!" Grey growled.

"Well, that sounds like bullshit," Raina offered, disgruntled. "Grey, I'm going to call the PT over at Silver Creek and have him come on out. Those guys are Grey's size and bigger, and he's done phenomenal work. I'll text you and let you know when he can come."

And before Lily could say anything else, Raina had taken off up the path around the cottage. She and Grey stared at each other awkwardly.

"Would you like a sandwich? I didn't make them, but it's the least I can do for everything you've done today... Everything."

"I–I should go Lily, let you and Caleb get some rest. I'll be back with some of the guys to finish up. Is nine okay?"

Lily swallowed a surprising amount of disappointment and nodded.

Grey looked like he was going to say something else, but turned his focus to her phone. "Put in my number in case you need anything."

"Grey, I quit."

"Lily, Ivy comes home in a month. I figured this is the

best place to be to prepare for that. Plus, I didn't accept your resignation and your contract requires you to work to the end of the term except in case of dire injury."

She had no intentions of leaving, not when Ivy would be a hop and skip away. Shoot, she'd move herself and Caleb in her baby's room if she didn't think it would be creepy for the kid. But still...

"You don't like me deciding for you," he said, reading her mind.

"My contract also states unfavorable working relationships and this..."

"Is workable," he stated flatly. "We are both adults, with a child together. Finish your contract and that frees us both up to focus on our kids and our students."

She noticed he said 'our kids,' and she appreciated him thinking of Caleb.

Grrr...

Her phone buzzed in her hand, and Ivy's face popped up, making a duck face. Her heart stopped. Six more photos came in rapid succession as Greyson walked into the night.

"This discussion is not over," she whispered to his back.

* * *

THE NEXT DAY, the late afternoon sun dipped behind the hills, casting a beautiful glow over the ranch. Dust swirled around Lily and Greyson as they stared at the half-assembled swinging bench before them. A late arrival, the bench was the perfect addition among the flowers off the back porch and she couldn't wait to see it set up. She could see students gathering there, bonding over music.

The men from Silver Creek had already left. They were

nice and hardworking. Cashea was hilarious, and she'd truly enjoyed their company. Cashea made her promise to come out to the local bar - the Hen House - on Fridays for a good time.

Going out always carried a risk of being recognized, but she figured the chances were small. It was times like this she was happy her alter ego, LaLa Fair, was such a different person and personality than Lily. And with her voice trashed...LaLa was fading further from her real life. She wasn't sure how she felt about that.

"Okay," Lily said, planting her hands on her hips. "We lift on three. I'll balance it with my good leg, and you... well, you just don't drop it."

Greyson rolled his eyes. "Thanks for the vote of confidence."

They both bent down to lift the large wooden beam. Lily gritted her teeth against the pain in her leg while Greyson struggled with the stiffness in his left arm. As they tried to maneuver the heavy piece into place, his grip faltered.

The bench slipped from his hands and landed in the dirt with a loud thud. Before either of them could react, the weight of the beam shifted, tipping sideways and sending a wave of muddy water from a nearby puddle splashing all over both of them.

For a moment, they stood there in stunned silence, mud dripping down their faces and clothes.

Then Lily snorted.

She tried to hold it in, but what was the point? She shook with giggles.

"You're laughing?" Greyson asked, wiping mud off his face with an annoyed swipe of his hand.

Lily doubled over, gasping for breath between laughs. "I'm sorry... but that? *That* was funny!"

Greyson's mouth twitched, and despite himself, he let out a small chuckle.

She shook her head, still grinning. "I think the bench wins. I give up."

As her laughter died down, she noticed the hard set of Greyson's jaw. He rubbed at his left arm, his frustration evident. "It's my fault," he muttered. "I still feel like half the man—"

"Stop." Lily cut him off, her voice soft but firm. "You're not half of anything. This ranch is a lot of work for anyone, that bench is heavy as hell, and we're both a little, well, a lot banged up. That doesn't make you any less."

Greyson glanced away, jaw tight. "You don't know what it's like. Every day it's a reminder that I'll never be the man I used to be."

Lily's smile faded, replaced by a quiet empathy. She gently touched his arm and led him to the back porch steps. He held her hand as she lowered herself onto the step, then he sat down roughly. "I *do* know... So, IED?" she asked gently.

For a moment, he said nothing, staring out at the horizon as the memories washed over him. "The explosion took out half the convoy, and the rest of us... were trapped. There was fuel everywhere and the whole thing just went up in flames."

He paused, his dark brown eyes growing distant as he relived the nightmare. "We managed to pull a few guys out... Not everyone could be saved... The fire spread so fast, and I got caught in it. Burns covered half my body by the time they got me out."

Lily's heart ached at the pain in his voice. She reached

out, hesitating for just a moment before placing her hand lightly on his good arm. "I'm so sorry, Greyson."

He studied her. "I've been through therapy; done everything I'm supposed to. But it doesn't change the fact that this,"—he gestured to the burns on his arm and chest and down to his unseen legs—"is who I am now. And no amount of ranch work or pretending otherwise is going to change that."

Lily sat quietly beside him, the mud drying on them as she absorbed his words. "You're not defined by your scars," she said softly. "You're still here. Still fighting. And that counts for something."

Greyson huffed a short, humorless laugh. "You sound like my therapist."

"You can't afford me," she teased lightly, giving him a small smile. "You're already getting a deal for the students... Listen, we've all got scars, Grey. Life is an ass kicker, the scars, the changes, show we're still in this."

He considered her for a moment, then his gaze flickered to her leg, and the limp she couldn't hide, especially the last two days. His expression softened. "What about you?" he asked quietly. "The accident left you... with more than meets the eye, huh?"

Lily's smile faltered as her eyes found purchase on the ground. "I—" she started, but the words seemed to catch in her throat.

Greyson's brows furrowed in concern. "Lily—"

"I'm not ready to talk about it," she cut him off, her voice tight. She swallowed hard, blinking away the all too familiar sting in her eyes. "Not yet. You know I used to have a *beautiful* body. Thick and smooth like silk. Now...well parts of me look more like crushed velvet. No more mini skirts." She shrugged.

Greyson nodded slowly. "Okay. Whenever you're ready."

Lily gave him a small, grateful nod. Silence stretched between them again, but it wasn't as uncomfortable as before. They sat side by side, both broken in their own ways, both quietly understanding that their wounds, all of them, would take time.

Finally, Greyson stood, attempting to brush the dirt and mud from his pants. "We should get this bench finished before midnight."

"You're not taking my resignation on that either, huh?" Lily shook her head and took his outstretched hand, wincing slightly as she rose to her feet. "Ok...let's cool it on the mud baths this time. My face is already flawless."

He smirked, the tension between them softening. "No promises."

9

SONGBIRD

GREYSON

LILY DISAPPEARED INTO THE OUTDOOR SHOWER NEAR her cottage, her hair and clothes caked in mud.

The look on her face when the bench collapsed was priceless, but the look on her face, the pride, when they finished it together? Angelic.

He remembered that face. He was starting to remember a lot of things.

As the water began to run, he leaned back against the porch railing, still smiling to himself. The humor of the situation had done something to ease the tension between them. Maybe it was the absurdity of it all, or maybe it was something deeper—something he wasn't ready to admit yet.

Suddenly, a loud scream cut through the night air.

Without a second thought, Greyson bolted to the shower, heart pounding as he yanked open the door. "Lily!"

She was naked under the cold spray, her eyes wide in

shock, hands frantically trying to turn off the water. "It's freezing! I tried to turn it off, but the tap—"

He saw it immediately: the handle had snapped off in her hands. Water sprayed everywhere, and before he could think, he was under the shower with her trying to control the flood. His clothing was soaked, sticking to his skin as icy water drenched them both.

"Damn it," he muttered, maneuvering his body to block the spray as best he could. His back took the brunt of the freezing water while he fumbled with the emergency shutoff valve.

Lily laughed through her teeth chattering, watching him fight the spray like it was a battle in itself. "If I-I-I didn't know better, I'd think you were s-s-setting me up," she quipped, a smirk tugging at the corner of her lips. "The bench and now this-s-s-s..."

Greyson finally managed to shut the water off, the sudden silence very loud. He turned to her, dripping wet and breathless...very aware of the naked woman in front of him. "I wouldn't hurt you, Songbird."

She froze, the playful smirk slipping from her face as his old nickname for her fell from his lips as if he'd never stopped saying it. His heart ached at the sound of it and he could tell it affected her too. Her voice was quieter when she responded, her eyes meeting his. "But you did, Greyson."

His face paled as the weight of her words settled between them. He took a step closer, shaking his head slowly. "I didn't know, Bird. I loved you so darlin'... And I was grateful for every moment near you and understood I didn't deserve it. When I thought you left..." His voice cracked, the regret so raw in his tone that it sent a shiver down her spine.

He grabbed the towel hanging nearby and gently wrapped it around her trembling shoulders, his hands lingering as he rubbed her arms, trying to stop the shivering. He touched her gently, afraid she'd break under his big, clumsy hands.

The space between them was electric, their breaths mingling in the cool night air. His dark eyes searched hers, and there was no anger—only the sharp relief of pain and a hint of wonder.

"I thought I was throwin' rocks at the sun..." he started, but the words hung in the air unfinished.

She swallowed hard, her pulse quickening as his hands slid up to cup her face, his thumb brushing away a droplet of water from her cheek. Her heart strummed beneath his arm as the silence stretched between them, unspoken words heavy in the air. He held himself back for moments that stretched for forever until she tipped her face up to him in permission, in askance, in submission.

And he closed the distance.

His lips pressed against hers, soft and searching, tentative at first, as he refamiliarized himself with her taste. Then she kissed him back and something inside them broke free.

It wasn't just a kiss. It was pain and missed moments. Darkness and contrition. It was an apology, a confession, a moment long overdue.

For a brief time, the world fell away. There was no ranch, no trauma, no mistakes of their past—only the feeling of her wrapped in his arms. Her softness pressing against him, making him feel alive again.

Whole again.

After long breathless moments they broke apart, their foreheads resting against each other, reality sinking in.

"Grey..." she whispered, "We can't."

She unbuttoned buttons of his shirt. "Things are too complicated."

He reached out, slid the lock on the door, and returned to gripping her at the waist and hip, kneading the soft, ample flesh as a satisfied groan escaped his throat. He'd missed the lushness of her.

"Complicated," he echoed as Lily kissed his neck and his skin - both healing and undamaged - as she pulled back his shirt.

"We have to be responsible," she whispered.

"We will," he whispered into her neck as he lifted her leg at the thigh and rested her foot on the little stool off to the side, opening her to him. Holding her firm he captured her mouth again and reached for her wet washcloth on the hook breaking the kiss only long enough to thoroughly wipe his face.

"Hold your pussy open for me Songbird," he said quietly into her ear, aware of how close they were to the cottage. "My hands are filthy."

"So is your mouth," she panted.

"If I remember correctly, you like that." He grinned against her throat as she did what she was told. He collapsed to his knees in prayer to her temple as she invited him to worship her.

"Keep her just like that," he moaned into her wetness and began to drag his tongue through her pussy and over her clit. A small thunk accompanied her head falling back against the wall of the tiny shower. They were wedged in there tight with barely enough room to breathe let alone fuck, but who needed breathin' when he had his Songbird swirling her hips against his face?

He held her hips to him when she started to scoot away, the sensations taking over her body, her quiet gasps spurring him on as he sucked on her clit. Her first orgasm hit her hard and he was rewarded with a rush of her desire that he eagerly lapped up. She made him ravenous. Her smell, the sight of her open for him, the softness of her thighs... He turned and placed a tight little bite on the nearest and she squeaked then moaned as he soothed the bite with ministrations of his tongue. As she came down from her orgasm she let go of herself.

"Hands back on the pussy Songbird," he growled into her thigh.

"But–"

He nipped her thigh again. And she squeaked again before obeying.

"Good girl."

He grinned as a fresh waterfall of her accompanied his praise and he made sure not to waste a single drop. She made him feel ten feet tall with her soft "Yes baby," "Please baby," and "Grey baby, yes."

He'd feasted so long his knees were screaming, but he'd handled worse with much less reward and he determined he would lick, suck and tongue fuck his little songbird until she begged him to stop.

Which she did, eventually. She was shaking and limp by the time he placed soft kisses on her hands, on her pussy itself, on her inner thigh, then her hip of her leg, as he lowered it. He kissed the hip of her injured leg noting the scarring running the length. Some looked surgical, others looks like skin had been ripped away in chunks and filled back in and his heart hurt for her all over again.

He kissed his way up her leg, over every scar he found, back to her hip, across her soft, rounded stomach, up and across her chest... his bad arm shook with the effort it took to raise himself up and support her, but he was determined to take the time needed to properly care for her.

He ended his ministrations lingering at her mouth. "Can you walk?"

She searched his eyes before nodding.

"Then let's get you in the house so you can properly clean up."

"Grey..." Her eyes dropped to his mouth and back to his eyes. "I don't– We never brought men around Caleb, not since that article about the threesome came out and this is–"

"Complicated. I know Songbird. I just want to make sure you're taken care of, not angling for a sleepover."

"Oh."

He grabbed her ass with both his hands and pulled her tight to him. "Just a note sweetheart - never bring up another man while I still have the scent of you in my lungs and the taste of you on my tongue."

"One was a woman," she whispered, a wicked little smile on her face.

"Lily," he growled low against her mouth. "Go get cleaned up. Now."

* * *

LILY

She came out of sleep with the sense someone was watching her again.

She opened her eyes slowly and took in his bulky frame sitting in the chair by the window. He wanted her to see him and unlike the first time he let himself in the room, she had no desire to break his nose.

"Can't sleep?"

"I'm starving."

She was fully awake then. "Dude, did you really break into my room looking for a meal? I don't even cook like that. *Of all shit for a sexy ass Marine to say.*"

"Invite me to bed Songbird," Grey rumbled from his seat.

Oh...Be strong Lily.

"This is a bad idea Grey."

"It's a completely fucked up idea, Bird. We'll talk about it in therapy tomorrow. Now, invite me to bed so I can eat."

Call her an impetuous, wanton slut puppy - and she was, proudly - but she'd never been able to resist Grey when he used that tone. And the way he'd kissed her scars...

Whew.

She would regret this, they both would... but for now... She threw back the covers, slipped off her bonnet, and tucked it under her pillow. Pulling her oversized t-shirt off, she let him see all of her again by the soft moonlight. How she'd changed, how she'd stayed the same, her lumps, dimples and rolls. Everything.

It hadn't been easy to be a plus sized performer in this world but she'd taken society's arrows and made herself stronger. Her insecurities rested in the damaged parts of her, not the fat parts. And he devoured her with his eyes much like he would definitely do with his mouth again.

"Come to bed, baby."

* * *

GREY ROSE from the chair and she felt like prey. He stalked toward her and any thoughts she had about not feeling his powerful body against her died in the fire of her lust.

The man had always been gorgeous, but seeing him like this, in the way his time in the Marines and on the ranch changed him? Bigger, rougher, more...majestic.

He pulled off his shirt, toed off his shoes as he slid his joggers down over his hips and his manhood bobbed at attention. The shape was slightly different than she remembered.

He'd been burned there as well. Jesus.

"Don't pity me," he growled.

His accusation hurt. Didn't he know she would never...

"Why would I, should I pity you?" She gestured down her body at the patchwork of scaring and reconstruction. "You survived and all of you is beautiful. Grey...come..."

He hesitated only a moment more before sliding in next to her and claiming her mouth, sliding her injured leg over his hip and resting himself up against her. He ran a gentle, possessive hand over top of her scars and everywhere he touched sent sparks and activated damaged nerves in a different way. It wasn't long before she was reaching between them eager to feel him inside of her.

He stilled her hand. "Gentle. I'm more sensitive now.

And I've been tested. I've never been without protection with anyone, but you Songbird."

She nodded and softened her touch. "Same," she whispered. When his eyes went wide in surprise, she rolled hers in response. "Ninety percent of LaLa Fair stories are just that. The other ten percent are, well... a woman can have a healthy sex life and be responsible at the same time Grey— Oh God babeeee..."

He entered her and dipped his head to capture a nipple in his mouth, cutting her off mid mini rant. The sensation of him slowly long stroking her mixed with the emotions of her heart created a combustible concoction that she knew right then would destroy her in the long run.

"I told you 'bout talking about other men when I smell like you, I'm gonna have to fuck you until you remember I don't want to hear that shit darlin'."

And he did. Fuck yeah he did...

Grey was deliberate in his strokes, careful to angle himself so he'd have maximum contact with her clit, bringing her to heights again and again.

Because of his sensitivity, he had to get creative with extending his...efforts.

And it was fucking fantastic.

Rather than throwing off the rhythm, he teased and caressed, licked and sucked more. He paid *more* attention to her erogenous zones rather than relying on dicking her down.

He coo'd beautiful words she missed hearing.

He gripped her tummy, plumping it, and nipping at it before diving back into her heat.

He *was* starving and later, as she took him into the back

her mouth, she understood because she was ravenous. Ravenous for everything that was Grey.

Before she finally drifted off to sleep, he cleaned her with such care, and set up her pillows to support her leg. She had to bite her lip to keep from showing what his care meant to her.

Throwing the covers over the both of them, Grey set his alarm for an hour. Plenty of time to leave before Caleb woke, but in her heart of hearts she didn't want him to leave.

This was such a bad fucking idea.

* * *

LILY WATCHED from the porch as Greyson sat on the ground with Caleb under the shade of a large, old tree. It was early morning, and the ranch hummed with activity. Caleb adjusted the strings on a couple of the guitars she brought for student use. She was in the middle of careful preparations for the students' arrival, and the nervous mental chaos of trying to prepare to meet her daughter, but something about this moment made her pause.

Lily thought they were just talking about the ranch, but then she heard Caleb quietly ask, "Did you know my mom? What was she like back then?" and her chest tightened.

Marigold is...was... the light of her life, her sister, her best friend. Caleb rarely asked about her directly, preferring to keep his feelings locked away, or disclosed, she guessed, to his therapist. *This* interaction felt different. She hadn't expected him to reach out to Grey of all people.

Greyson shifted in the dirt, his expression softening as he looked at Caleb. "Yeah, buddy. I knew your mom well. We all went to school together."

Lily leaned against the wooden railing, reminding herself to breathe deeply as she watched them. Greyson's voice was low and calm, steadying Caleb.

"Your mom was... she was brilliant, kid. Smartest person in the room, no matter where she went. She had a brain for numbers that I'd never seen before. Where Lily and I struggled with our maths, for her it was a game. She sang all the time just like Lily. And I know you know, their voices together? Magic. She never got jealous like some siblings would have when your aunt performed. Music was more... personal for her. To be enjoyed and shared just with those who mattered."

Grey tapped his hand against his leg. "I missed her friendship a lot over the years. She was honest, exceptionally kind, and the best thing about her? How much she loved you. She read to her tummy, to you, all the time. She even put headphones on her belly so you could hear all the best music. Classical for sure, but also jazz, rock, hip hop, international... She lived for you."

Caleb blinked up at Greyson. "Did she ever talk about my dad?" His voice wavered, a little crack of vulnerability slipping through.

Lily stiffened. Caleb had never asked her about his father—not like this. Marigold was always honest with him, explaining that his father was someone who couldn't handle responsibility, who hadn't wanted to be a part of their lives. She never hid the truth, so Lily was surprised to hear Caleb express curiosity now.

Greyson hesitated, his jaw tightening slightly. He glanced briefly toward her, sensing her presence and she straightened, her body tensing with anticipation of needing to step in.

"Your dad..." Greyson started slowly, his voice taking on a harder edge. "He wasn't a good man, Caleb. He wasn't someone who deserved your mom or you. He hurt her in ways that weren't fair."

Caleb frowned. "Why didn't he want us?"

Greyson's eyes softened again. "That was his failure. Not yours, and not your mom's. She deserved better, the best kind of love and so do you." He paused, glancing over at Lily for a moment before continuing, his tone darker. "And I made sure he knew that."

Lily's stomach flipped. She stepped down from the porch, crossing over to them. "What do you mean?"

Grey didn't look at her at first, keeping his focus on Caleb. "He was making things hard on her... So I made sure he wasn't a problem for the family anymore."

Caleb tilted his head, cautious curiosity in his eyes. "What did you do?"

Lily's twisted her ring, for some reason unable to take it off. There had been rumors, whispers of something happening with Marigold's professor, but her sister never confirmed it.

Greyson finally looked up at Lily, his eyes clouded with a mix of guilt and something she hadn't seen before—a hardened fierceness. "I whupped his ass, Songbird," he said quietly. "The shit he was saying to her, fucking with her classes... I couldn't watch him hurt her anymore, so I made sure he couldn't."

Lily blinked, wrapping her mind around what he confessed. She never knew. She hadn't realized just how far Greyson had gone to protect her sister, nor what she had dealt with. It was something Marigold kept to herself and, in fact, took to her grave.

Lily's heart swelled, a warmth growing inside her as she watched Greyson with her nephew. She hadn't expected this —hadn't expected to feel anything other than the old resentment she'd carried toward him. But seeing him here, like this, caring for Caleb in ways she hadn't known he was capable of, gave her insight to the kind of father he must be to Ivy. She'd missed out on seeing that growth in him, but Ivy hadn't and damn, she was grateful for it.

"He never bothered her again after that," Greyson continued, turning back to Caleb. "Your mom was strong, buddy. She didn't let him stop her from living her life or loving you."

Caleb stared down at the ground, silent for a moment. "She was *really* smart. When Auntie Lily toured, she always took us with her and Mom was my homeschool teacher. She knew everything. Every city there was some lesson or tour and Auntie always made sure we got to see the stuff other people didn't see. Like personal tours of Stradivarius violin vaults."

"My daughter has been in some of the best boarding schools in the country," Greyson said softly. "And I would've sent her to study with your mom in a heartbeat. She almost always treated me well."

"Almost?"

"Well, there was the time I said I had four books and a possible in Spades and barely got two..."

Lily barked out a loud laugh at that. She remembered. They lost first round of the Spades tournament in grad school and Mari was so mad she dogged Grey for two weeks. Lily stayed out of it. Mari already knew Lily's brain was music, history, the arts - not cards.

"And the other time?" she asked smiling, thinking he

would talk about the time he ate a whole pan of brownies an eight month pregnant Mari made to satisfy a craving. Exhausted by the effort, Mari fell asleep and when she woke, Grey was shaking crumbs from the pan into his mouth while watching car races.

"When she learned I hurt you. She took my call once, called me a hypocrite, and hung up. It makes a lot more sense now."

Lily nodded, her throat tight. She sat next to Caleb, who rested his head on her shoulder.

"I think she would've loved that Auntie Lily broke your nose."

Their laughter together carried on the wind across the flatlands of the ranch. It sounded a lot like new beginnings.

10

ANCHOR ME

GREYSON

Lily and Greyson entered the dimly lit Hen House, the sounds of laughter, a DJ, clinking glasses, and hoots over the various sports on the TV screens greeting them.

"I haven't played darts in ages," Lily said, her eyes lighting up at the dartboard on the far wall.

"Let's see if you still suck at it," Grey replied, a playful smirk on his face. He grabbed a set of darts from the wall, handing three to her.

Lily stepped up to the line and focused intently on the board, taking a deep breath before throwing. The dart landed with a satisfying thud, just nowhere near the board.

"Duck!" Greyson shouted with a laugh. There was no one close enough to hit, but he enjoyed messing with her, anyway. He tossed his dart with flair, landing it closer to the center.

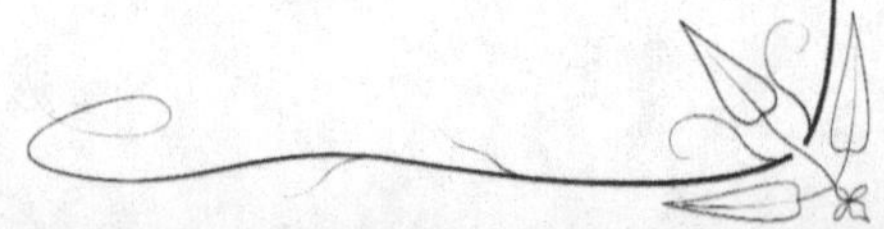

Several rounds of darts and a couple of beers later, they were laughing more than they were playing.

"Shit. Why did I ever think this was fun?" she asked, breathless.

"Because you always bet your ass, I would win and fuck you in the bathroom." His gaze turned serious, and the air between them grew heavy with desire.

Before she could respond, Greyson took her hand, leading her through the crowd towards the restroom. "But I didn't bet anything," she protested, while her feet in her long boots had no problem keeping up. She'd already started moving better since working with the Silver Creek physical therapist. Turns out she didn't have to be a hundred and sixteen pounds to walk better. She just needed someone who paid attention to her actual body, not the weight in her chart.

His heart felt light, giddy even, at the progress they made - individually and together - as people and for the ranch. Caleb was talking about Mari more and coming further out of his shell.

He caught a smirk and hat tip from Draven as they passed his designated Friday night spot at the bar.

The small bathroom was empty, the sound of their laughter echoing off the walls. As soon as they stepped inside, Greyson shut the door behind them, leaning against it. Her gaze turned hungry, and he pulled her to him by her waist.

"This is a bad idea," Lily said, half-laughing, half-nervous.

"You say that every time," he replied and pulled up her long, flowing skirt until he had access to her panties and slid them down. "Yet, you're already wet."

With that, he tipped her head back and claimed her

mouth with a deep, passionate kiss. She opened to him and he dove in, their tongues search and tasting. Greyson pulled the scoop neck of her shirt lower, biting little love nips along her breasts as she pressed in closer, desperate to feel more of him. He dropped to his knees and forced his shoulders between her legs, spreading her wide for him.

"Grey, baby," she murmured, rocking her pelvis against his lips, the rest of her words lost to moans as he sucked her clit. Mindful of time, he turned, pulled her to the sink, and pressed her forward, dipping just low enough to catch his dick at her entrance. He lifted her chin and spoke to her through the mirror.

"Let me see that pretty face as you take all of me, darlin.'"

The smile on her face, the way she bit her bottom lip as he slid in to the hilt, the bead of sweat dripped down between her breasts... she was stunning.

"Such a bad idea," he whispered to her in the mirror.

"Mmm, the worst."

"Be even worse if you creamed all over me and I had to walk around smelling like you."

That turned her on even more and she fucked him back, the sound of their explosive coupling echoing off the walls. Sliding his hand up the back of her head and burying it in her free 'fro of curls, he used the leverage to stroker even deeper, using his free hand to give her the stimulation she needed to explode and when she lit up, it was stu-fucking-pendous.

His name on her lips, her mouth open in desire, and being buried inside her? He could have died right then and in fact he thought he did, coming so hard his heartbeat roared in his ears.

Afterward, he helped her with her clothes as she peppered him with kisses. "Well, that was..."

"A terrible idea," Greyson finished, a grin playing on his lips.

"Awful," she agreed, trying to regain her composure. "...you're coming by tonight, right?"

"Doubling down," he said, his expression softening.

"Right," she replied, biting her lip as they both shared a knowing look.

With a final shared smile, they left the restroom, stepping back into the noise of the bar, the thrill of the moment lingering in the air.

* * *

LILY

Cashea and her cover band were awesome. Her voice was clear and sweet when it needed to be, sinful and dark when the emotions took her there... It had been a long time since Lily just enjoyed live music. If she wasn't scouting for background singers, she was scoping out writing talent.

This was plain fun. Cashea and the crowd were having a good time and the heat between her and her man Draven was palpable as she sang *for* everyone, but only *to* him.

"Do you miss it?"

She pretended she didn't hear him.

"I know you heard me."

She snorted and rolled her eyes at him. Glancing around, she leaned into him to be sure he could hear her and no one overheard. "Sometimes. I miss singing. I miss the crowd grooving along with you, connecting. I don't miss the alter ego or the constant touring. I sure as fuck don't miss the tour bus."

"Would you go back?"

"Of course, it's what I do."

She felt him stiffen beside her and she met his stare head on. "You said it yourself, traveling the world is a great education for kids. Lily and Caleb will hopefully get along well together and while it's not going to be the same without...without Mari; I can hire the best teachers for them as they *experience* history, languages, and science."

Grey sat back, staring at her. "Sounds like you got it all figured out. What about me?"

She sighed, shaking her head. "I have nothing figured out, and you'd always be welcome to join us."

"Welcome to... I'm not some fucking stagehand–"

"Grey, calm down." She looked around, making sure everyone's attention was elsewhere. "You're getting upset about hypotheticals–"

"I'm pissed about possibilities, Bird. You can't just take my daughter–"

"*Our* daughter. And what? You expect me to only drop by when a tour moves through after I've lost ten years with her? She goes to boarding school for chrissakes. It's not like you see her for breakfast every morning."

"*I was deployed,*" he growled.

"*And I don't judge you for YOUR job.*"

"Now let's slow things down with a little love song," Cashea raised voice crooned from the stage as she looked in their direction.

Shit, they were being rude as hell. She adjusted in her seat, the ache in her movement reminding her of their moments not too long before. The opening notes to LaLa

Fair's first number one song "Anchor Me," started and how the fuck was this her life?

All the letters I never wrote,
Tattooed in my heart for you
All the heartbeats I ever felt
Anchored me to you

Lily sat through Cashea's beautiful version of her song, loving the key changes and harmony while also hating the absolutely worse fucking timing. Grey stewed next to her and the song she wrote at the height of her postpartum depression about the loves she'd lost - Greyson and Ivy - played for what felt like the entire world. As LaLa Fair, she had armor. She was another person. As Lily she was politely bleeding out note after note.

"I hate this fucking song," Greyson grumbled.

*And..*she was out. She normally didn't leave during someone's set, but it was that or shank a fucker with a beer bottle.

Standing, she blew Cashea a kiss, turned to Grey, and leaned in to make sure he heard every fucking word she said.

"I wrote this when I had PPD so deep my family wanted to put me on suicide watch. Music, of course, helped heal me. Helped me scratch out the thoughts itching my head about the two heartbeats outside of me, gone forever - you and Ivy. Helped me carve out how I was forever anchored to you. Helped me wish that someday, somewhere, you'd hear it and hear my heart calling to you."

* * *

DID *that say three hours until a rideshare?* Lily backed out of the app and opened it again.

Fucking South Dakota.

"Hey beautiful, glad to see you ditch that jacked up asshole. I can give you a ride."

Not bothering to look up, Lily shook her head. "I'm good, honey, thanks."

"I know you *have* to be," the voice said, too fucking close all of a sudden.

Shit. How did that happen?

Lily looked over her shoulder in time to see the man attached to the voice yanked up and back by some invisible force.

Fucking Grey.

Sure enough, Greyson quickly threw a booted foot on the man's chest while leaning in, saying something that was surely illegal in most countries.

"Get in the truck Lily."

"Grey."

"You're outside a bar, by yourself at night, staring at your goddamn phone, not using the sense that God gave you because you're pissed off at me. And now I gotta kill a fucker unless you. GET. IN. THE. TRUCK."

"What?!" she said with an attitude.

"What?!" the man on the ground yelped in shock.

He was a pain in the ass. "*Grrr...*" Turning, she limp stomped to his truck and waited at the back door.

"I'm not your goddamn chauffeur."

"I'm getting in the fucking car. You either take the win or kill a fucker."

"Ma'am, get in the front please," the man, still on the ground, still with a boot over his heart, said.

"You better confess your sins, homie, because either I sit back here or he and I are both going to jail tonight."

Greyson hit his remote, and she climbed into the backseat.

Whoo hoo extended cabs.

When he finally got in the truck, she stopped him before he started.

"Don't say a fucking word."

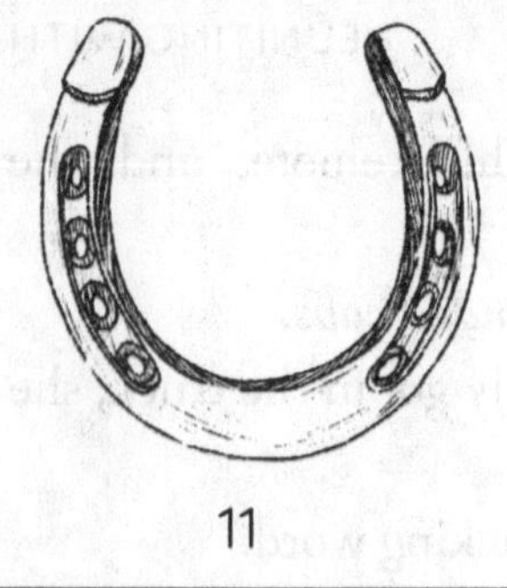

11

QUITE THE TEAM

GREYSON

"Oh, my god you two are having sex."

Their third session that week with the therapist did not go as well as previous sessions. In the time they'd learned the truth, or at least part of it, their three times a week therapy sessions centered on navigating their feelings and breaking the news to Ivy. It was good. Productive. He was hopeful about their future.

Then last night at the bar happened and now, this morning's session was a fucking disaster with his mother.

Ivy was coming home early because of a measles outbreak at her school, which meant he had to fly his mother out this morning, have her sign Lily's NDA and start the confrontation now. Ivy was set to arrive later that evening. The slow, intentional build up was now a massive diarrhea slide.

And his mother had somehow sniffed out the one thing they hadn't disclosed to the therapist.

"Is this true, Grey? Lily?" Dr. Riley asked the two of them, his eyebrows raised.

"Not anymore," Lily replied.

"Oh my god, no wonder he had to raise Ivy alone. She's inconsistent!"

"Mom. Enough." Grey glared at her. He loved his mother, but he was still processing what she did and what it meant for all of them. "Lily and I started a relationship shortly after she arrived at Crystal Fountain."

"Doesn't waste any time, does she?"

"You've got one more time to say something disrespectful about the mother of my child after what you put her through. This is about Ivy first, Lily and my relationship second, and finding a way forward for you, Ivy and me, Mom. But I swear on everything, you have got to stop this!"

"I'm sorry, a way forward?" Lily sputtered. "With what? An arrest? Medication? In person treatment? I don't want this woman anywhere near Ivy for the rest of her childhood. If she decides as an adult to engage, I'll have to respect her decision, but my child is not safe around her!"

"I *raised* your child while you were off gallivanting, gyrating, and being coked up as 'LaLa Fair.' Now that you've been humbled," Mrs. Monroe glanced at Lily's cane, "NOW you want to be a mother."

"YOU TOLD ME MY CHILD WAS DEAD! You gave me ashes that I have worn for a decade! Buried my mother, my sister with because what? I wanted to have an at home birth? Grey fell in love with me? This is, clinically, nuts and I can't do it," she said, her voice growing hoarse. "YOU manipulated me into signing papers, relieving me of my rights, telling me they were discharge papers. YOU told me Greyson blamed me for our child dying and didn't want to see me again. YOU continue to lie and manipulate to this day. I do not want you in Ivy's life. This is a hard boundary. I want my rights back, shared custody, and I want to know who the hell is buried with my mother?!"

"Oh, don't be so dramatic. It's Greyson's father Douglas. He'd be thrilled to be buried with a Black woman. Greyson takes after him."

Well, that took a hard left into what the fuck.

"Mrs. Monroe," Dr. Riley interrupted, "if you have any hope of continuing a relationship with your son and maybe your granddaughter, there are some difficult things you must confront. Dr. Belmont wants answers to reasonable questions."

"*Doctor* Belmont was practically a teen, starting a family on childish whims like her sister. Ivy suffered for those decisions. She was a poor, sick little thing and Greyson, he was beside himself. He had a bright future ahead of him and my little boy was now saddled with a sick baby and a fiancé who couldn't properly care for her. Their breakup was bound to happen. I was being a good mom, saving my son the heartache and legal issues in the future. I always wanted a little girl, and I was happy to step in and help Greyson raise her. We are quite a team."

His mother tucked her graying hair behind her ear, satisfied that she'd given a perfectly normal answer.

"Yep. That'll do it," Lily said, leaving without looking back.

* * *

LILY

She paced back and forth in the living room, her heart

racing as she cracked her knuckles. The air was on full blast, but she was sweating like she was Grey's daddy at Essence Fest.

She snorted. *So inappropriate.*

She hadn't removed her ring. It felt disrespectful to not do something positive with it.

"What if she hates me?" she blurted out, touching her hand to her hair. "I think I should have rewashed my hair. Day three wash and go can be tricky…"

Caleb sat on the couch playing a video game and paused it to raise an eyebrow. "You've only just meeting, and you're already worrying about that?"

"What if she thinks I'm ugly? What if she changed her mind about wanting to see me?" Lily's voice climbed an octave with each question. "What if she hates my music? I mean, she's probably only heard the songs as LaLa Fair. What if she doesn't even like Lily?"

Caleb chuckled, "That's a lot of 'what ifs' for one minute. You sound like you're about to crash out."

"Is she going to call me 'Mom' or just 'Lily'? What if she calls me 'Lils'? I hate when people shorten my name! Should I pretend to like it?" Lily pressed a hand to her forehead, her mind spinning. "I mean, I'm wearing purple, her favorite color. What if she thinks I'm trying too hard? Who am I to have a kid? I barely remember when it's time to eat!"

Caleb laughed, leaning back in his seat. "Tell me about it! But you have your alarms now. You're good Auntie."

Lily pulled out her phone, ready to set a dozen more alarms when Greyson stepped into the room, concern etched across his face. He approached her and gently took the phone from her hands. "Hey, let's take a breath first, okay?"

"But what if—"

"No 'what ifs.' Just focus on the moment. Ivy is excited to meet you, I promise," Greyson reassured her, his voice calming and steady.

No matter what their relationship was, she trusted him in that moment.

Caleb jumped up, pretending to act like her personal hype man. "You've got this, Auntie! Just remember, she's just a kid! And if she hates you, I'll just bribe her with video games and snacks."

Lily couldn't help but laugh, the tension easing a little. "You think that'll work?"

Caleb grinned mischievously. "Yep! You'll have a second broke best friend in no time."

With a deep breath, Lily nodded. The door opened, and Ivy stepped inside, her dark eyes bright with curiosity and hesitation. Lily's breath hitched in her throat.

She was even more *beautiful* in person. And tall! Already past Lily's shoulders. Her long braids were pulled back, and she wore a jumbo hoodie and leggings, making her look like any other preteen. However, she was not any other preteen. Ivy was *her* baby.

Ivy slipped off her shoes and looked at Greyson, who nodded encouragingly.

"Hi, Ivy," Lily managed to say, her voice trembling with a mix of excitement and fear.

Ivy tilted her head, studying her mother with wide eyes, and then broke into a smile. "You're wearing purple! That's my favorite color!"

Lily's heart soared at the recognition, and she found herself smiling back. "I wanted you to know I was thinking of you."

Ivy's grin widened, and in that moment, all of Lily's worries melted away. "I like your hair too. It eats." Ivy nodded approvingly.

Lily laughed. "Thank you. I like it better than the blonde."

Ivy nodded. "This is more, you. The other look is like an avatar."

Lily grinned even bigger. "Exactly. LaLa is my avatar!"

They all laughed for a moment and as it petered out, Lily grew nervous. She didn't know what to do with her hands and she didn't want to move too soon.

"Hey Ivy, I'm your cousin Caleb," he said as he opened his arms for a hug and she immediately allowed him to fold her in. For the first time in her life, Lily was jealous of her nephew.

"I'm the reigning Tetris king and I can show you all the ways to beat Auntie Lily."

Ivy laughed, her eyes settling back on her. "Could I maybe, hug you?"

"Oh God, yes please," Lily said immediately, and was rewarded with the sweetest hug she'd ever experienced. They stood like that for long moments, Lily absorbing Ivy's warmth, her presence, her very essence into her soul. Before she knew it, she'd soaked Ivy in her tears. "My sweet baby, I missed you for so long."

Ivy squeezed her tighter. "I missed you too—Mom."

Somewhere, beneath the ashes of the life torn from her, Lily felt something new bloom. And she would protect this new blossom with everything she had in her.

"All the letters I never wrote," Lily whispered as she took Ivy's face in her hands, wiping the tears that streamed down her sweet girl's face. "Tattooed in my heart for you. All the heartbeats I ever felt. Anchored me to you."

"I'm anchored, safe somewhere with you," Ivy whispered back. "Somewhere in my dreams, I'm anchored to you."

12

BLACKBIRD

GREYSON - A WEEK LATER

GREYSON STOOD AT THE EDGE OF LILY'S LIVING ROOM, scratching his growing in beard.

It gave him something to do with his hands as he watched Lily fuss over the kids. It had become their evening routine.

Ivy curled up on the couch next to Caleb, her eyes drinking in her mother's every step, like she was afraid she'd disappear. Caleb kept distracting her, showing her how to play different chords, patiently adjusting her fingers and encouraging his little cousin.

They'd eaten every meal together, gone for long walks and horseback rides with all four of them or different configurations of their...family? Greyson didn't know where he and Lily stood and for the kids, she was her usual self, but there was distance and awkwardness whenever they were alone. He decided to get time with Lily soon. The distance killed him and he knew she was hurting too.

Ivy tried to sing along with a higher note and Lily sat on the coffee table in front of her, pressing her hand to Ivy's belly and the note came out stronger and louder. Ivy's eyes popped in surprise and a smile lit up her face. "Is that how you learned to sing?"

"Sweet love, I was born singin', but I *worked* on getting better and it all starts here." She placed her hand on Ivy's torso again. "Beyonce used to run in heels singing - or at least that's the way the story goes. P!nk says she sings better upside-down, swinging in the air. Two things they have in common? Breath control and knowing how to use their diaphragm. It helps outside of singing too - when you're anxious or scared, or excited, controlling your breathing can help even you out."

"How about one song?" Greyson asked gently, his voice coaxing but careful, trying not to push too hard. "Just for us, Songbird. No audience, no pressure."

Ivy had hinted at this earlier, wanting to hear Lily's voice, even if just for a moment. The silence in the room thickened as Lily shifted uncomfortably. Her fingers twisted the edge of Ivy's blanket, and she shook her head slightly.

Caleb leaned in, whispering something to Ivy, and she smiled weakly before speaking.

"It's okay," she mumbled, not waiting for a response as she quickly got up.

Greyson rubbed the back of his neck, tension creeping up his spine. He reminded himself to give Lily room to navigate this.

"No, wait Ivy," she reached out to stop her. "I've asked you to trust me to show you who I am and so I'm going to trust you with really sensitive information... I don't know if I can sing," she finally said, her voice dropping to almost nothing before she cleared her throat and powered on.

Greyson frowned, confusion flickering across his face, the same look reflected in Ivy's. "What do you mean? Is it just nerves?"

Lily shook her head, her eyes on Ivy, her hand reaching for her Boogie Bear. "When my tour bus crashed... My sissy Marigold, and I were trapped inside. She was badly hurt and asked me to sing her to sleep and I did... I screamed for help and sang for her over and over for hours. Physically, they don't know if my throat will recover. Up here," she tapped her head, "and here," she tapped her heart, "I don't know if *that* will ever heal. I lost, *we* lost," she nodded to Caleb, who sat quietly staring at her, "big parts of us that night."

Greyson felt the weight of Lily's words crash down on him, his breath hitching as he processed the horror of it. He wanted to deny it, to make it better, but the truth hung heavy in the air. Her beautiful voice, a voice that brought him to tears many times before...Gone?

"Songbird," he whispered.

Lily sucked in a deep breath and shrugged. "More surgeries could work or... make it worse. Every time I open my mouth to vocalize or even try to hum, my voice just disappears. I'd sing you to the moon and back Ivy if I could."

Ivy slid off the couch and wrapped her arms around Lily. "Thank you for trusting me, Mom." Lily played with Ivy's fingers before bringing them to her lips to kiss.

Caleb starting picking out tunes quietly on the guitar, landing on Blackbird by the Beatles. Grey felt his throat tighten before he cleared it and started singing the song, with Ivy and Caleb joining in.

It was a song Mari and Lily loved, singing it daily to put

Caleb to bed back in the day. Lily sang the same song to Ivy in the womb, and he didn't have the heart to stop after she was born.

He sat next to her on the coffee table, grimacing when it groaned under his weight and took her hand in his. As they all sat together, the wind howling softly in the distance, Grey saw etched in her eyes all she'd had been through. The ghosts of her trauma swimming just behind like his own. His love for her, that constant swirling sea, swelled inside and crashed over him.

When they finished singing, he took her hand like she'd taken Ivy's and kissed it, placing it on his thigh.

"Boogie, lemme see that," he said, reaching out for the guitar. He fumbled a bit with position and made adjustments to compensate for his tighter muscles.

"You still play?" Lily looked at him in wonder.

He nodded. "There is a reason I looked for a music therapist for the kids. There's something about pouring into the notes..." And he started to sing "Iris."

* * *

LILY

The evening air was thick with unspoken tension as Lily stood on the back porch, a heaviness in her heart. Greyson leaned against the railing, watching her, his expression a mix of concern and confusion.

"Lily, can we talk about what's happening between us?" Greyson began, his voice low and cautious. "We're dancing around a lot, and it's time to address it."

Lily took a deep breath, steadying herself against the

railing. "I don't want to dance or dodge it anymore, Greyson. I need to be honest with you."

His brow furrowed, apprehension tightening his features. He stroked his beard to give his hands something to do. "Alright Songbird."

"I need to focus on Ivy and Caleb right now," she said, her voice trembling slightly. "After everything we've been through, they need me, us, more than ever. I can't let anything—or anyone—come between us again."

"Are you saying you want to throw what we were building away?" he asked, disbelief creeping into his tone. "Is that really what you want?"

"It's not about throwing this away; it's about prioritizing my kids," she clarified, her heart racing. "I'm scared, Greyson. Scared that if things don't work out between us, I'll lose Ivy again. I can't go through that kind of pain again."

His expression softened, but confusion lingered in his eyes. "But I thought we were building a family. We can do this together."

She shook her head, stepping back slightly, a barrier forming between them. "I need to feel secure in my relationship with Ivy. I want you to sign the paperwork reinstating my parental rights and agreeing to shared custody." She picked up the large envelope on the small wooden table, passing it to him.

Greyson's eyes widened in shock, and he felt a pang of hurt. "You really think I'd try to take her away from you?"

"No, but I need the assurance. If I'm going to move forward, I need to know my rights are protected," she explained, holding out the documents.

He hesitated for a moment, looking at the papers as if they held the weight of their entire relationship.

"I need you to understand how serious I am about this."

After a moment's hesitation, he took the papers and after looking them over closely; he signed them, his heart heavy. "I'll always support you and Ivy. You know that."

"Thank you," she whispered, relief washing over her, but quickly overshadowed by the gravity of what she was about to say next. "There's one more thing. I need you to agree to never allow your mother near us."

He stiffened, a flicker of defensiveness flashing across his face. "Lily... my mother—"

"Greyson, after everything she did, she's not well and hasn't been right for a long time," she interrupted, her voice firm. "If she'd do that to a twenty-five-year-old me, what will she do to a ten-year-old because it's what she believes is right? It's not just about us anymore."

He hesitated, the weight of his mother's influence pressing down on him. "I... I need time to think about that."

Lily's heart sank at his uncertainty. "This is about our children, Greyson. I can't compromise on this."

"I will always protect my family," he replied, his voice strained.

"Which one? Ivy and Caleb need us to be strong enough to make the tough decisions."

Greyson looked at her, his heart heavy with the reality of their situation. "You are *my* anchor, Lily. There is not a reality where I exist, and I don't have you in my heart. I've carried you with me in my soul, embedded in the marrow of who am ever since I first saw you walking across the quad. There is no choice, Songbird... It will always be you."

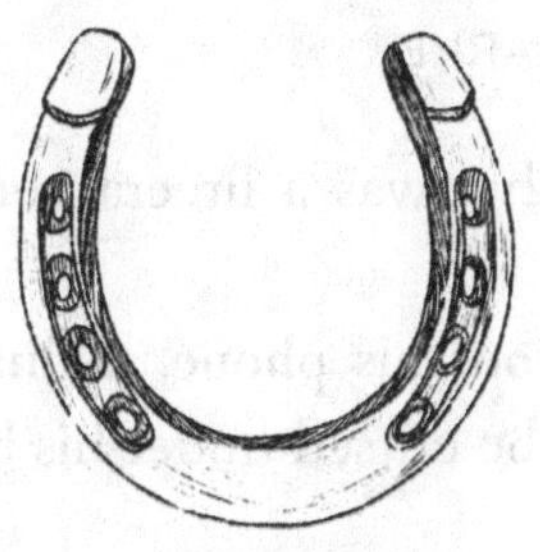

13

WINGS

LILY

She stood on the porch, her arms crossed tightly over her chest, her t-shirt damp against her skin as the wind picked up, blowing her curls every which way. Pulling her hair up into a bun, her skin prickled against the thick, humid air that always signaled a storm. The sky darkened far too quickly, and her gut twisted with unease.

Something wasn't right.

She slipped her sunglasses to the top of her head and turned to Grey, who stood by the truck, his face tense as he glanced up at the swirling clouds overhead.

"Have you seen the kids?"

He shook his head, frowning. "Not since Ivy came back from her session. I'll go check."

Lily's heart began to race, a sense of dread creeping up her spine. Ivy and Caleb had been inseparable since Ivy's return, but she could sense her daughter's struggles. The revelations about her true parentage were sometimes overwhelming, and Ivy was a firecracker of emotions, just like her.

Greyson pulled out his phone, dialing quickly. After a few tense moments, he cursed under his breath. "Neither of them is answerin'."

Lily's anxiety spiked. "We need to find them," she said, her voice tight. "The weather's turning."

As if to punctuate her words, a low rumble of thunder rolled across the sky. Lily grabbed her jacket and started for the truck, but before she could get inside, a voice called out from behind them.

It was Mrs. Monroe, her eyes wide with panic as she hurried toward them. "Ivy... she's upset," she said breathlessly. "She ran off... and Caleb followed."

Lily's heart fell out of her shoes. "Why are you here? What do you mean, ran off? Where did they go?!"

"I—I don't know," his mother stammered, her face pale. "I...I gave her more information about you just so she'd be informed. She got upset and ran off with Caleb."

A sick feeling churned in Lily's stomach. "What did you say to her?" she demanded, her voice rising. "What?!"

"I was just trying to explain," Greyson's mother replied, wringing her hands. "She asked about why I kept you away from her when she was little, and I—I told her things... things I thought she should know, that everyone already knows...the drugs and rehab, all the wild parties." She drew herself up and stared Lily in the eyes. "I told her the truth."

Lily hauled off and slapped the shit out of Mrs. Monroe, putting her full strength into the hit. The older woman fell on her ass in front of the truck with a loud cry.

"You told her lies from a pop star's PR machine rather than tell her YOU stole her life." She didn't have time for this shit. Lily ran around the hood of the truck, pushing past Grey to climb in. "You will burn in hell if anything happens to my babies and I will SEND YOU THERE."

Grey woke from whatever stupor in time to jump into the passenger seat as she floored it. She would later admit that, fortunately for all of them, Grey yanked the steering wheel to the right, making sure Lily avoided running over Mrs. Monroe, but it was millimeters close.

"Where would they go?" Lily asked Greyson. "The music room or the old barn? This storm's getting worse. We need to find them NOW."

Greyson clenched his fists, his jaw tight with rage. "The old barn by the creek," he said, his voice grim. "She'd associate the music room with you."

That hurt.

Lily pressed the pedal to the floor, racing along the ranch roads while the wind howled around them, whipping dust and debris into the air. The sky turned a sickly green, and Lily's heart raced faster with every passing second.

"They better be there," she muttered, gripping the steering wheel tightly. "They better be okay."

Greyson said nothing, his eyes focused straight ahead, but she could see the storm brewing inside him was just as fierce as the one outside.

When they reached the creek, she skidded to a stop, and both of them jumped out, running toward the old barn. The wind was so strong it nearly knocked Lily off her feet, painfully whipped her hair out of her bun, and wildly around her face. She kept pushing forward, ignoring the protests of her leg with her heart pounding in her ears.

"Ivy! Caleb!" she shouted, her voice barely audible to

her own ears over the roar of the wind. Between her yells and the dust, her throat felt like she'd swallowed glass.

Greyson was already at the barn door, yanking it open with a force that sent it swinging back wildly on its hinges. He looped a quick arm around her to pull her inside. Once her eyes adjusted, she saw them huddled in the corner, Caleb holding Ivy to him, their eyes wide with fear as the wind rattled the wooden structure.

A low growl rumbled across the sky as a funnel cloud touched down. It sounded just like people described it - a freight train. But not the tame, railroad crossing train, carefully tucked behind flashing lights and little barricades. No, this was as if the train was pissed off, coked out, and bearing down on them doing ninety in a school zone playing Death Metal. It had the kind of sound impact that reverberated through the body. The hand of God was delivering judgement on the whole of humanity and they were in a fucking barn.

Lily's heart pounded in her chest as the barn creaked under the pressure, the walls shaking, threatening to come apart at any moment. She pulled her babies to her while turning to make the dash back to the truck.

Greyson wrapped his arms around them all, his face grim as herded them into the center of the barn. "It's coming too fast. We won't make it to the truck." Without hesitating, Greyson shouted and motioned for them to "Lay down!" And with a great big heave, he pulled a large workbench over the top of them.

Lily pushed the kids down flat underneath the wide bench onto the floor. Caleb partially covered Ivy on one side. Lily tried covering them both with her trembling body, the intensity of the storm ratcheting up to hellish proportions.

Finally, Grey got under and used his body as the last barrier before the table, covering the kids' heads with one arm and hooking his other arm around her. His chest heaved with shallow breaths, and Lily could feel the weight of his fear. He brushed his lips brushing her ear. "I love you, Songbird," he yelled into her ear. "I love you Ivy, I love you Caleb!" he yelled into their huddle.

Tears leaked from her eyes as she squeezed them shut.

She was so fucking stupid.

Why hadn't she learned her lesson the first time or the second time she almost died? Grab love with both hands because it could disappear in a moment on the wind. Finally, in this moment, she understood—time had run out. Whatever they had, whatever they felt, this might be the last time to say it. "I never stopped," she yelled. "Never. Stopped. Loving you."

Greyson tightened his hold, pressing his forehead against hers as the tornado raged around them, tossing around debris around like straw, having a devastating impact on the walls of the barn. It continued to groan under the pressure; the wind screaming through the cracks in the walls. The kids yelled beneath them as the storm roared around them, violent and relentless, but they held on—together. Time stretched, every second was an eternity as they waited for the worst to pass.

Then suddenly, after years or mere moments, the wind died. The barn groaned one last time before falling silent, leaving behind only the sound of their ragged breathing and Ivy's quiet whimpers.

Lily lay there for a moment, her chest heaving as the adrenaline slowly ebbed, leaving her shaking and weak. She lifted her head, looking down at Ivy and Caleb. They were shaken and shaking, but alive—thank God, they were alive.

"We're okay," she whispered, more to herself than anyone else. "We're okay."

Greyson pulled her closer, his forehead still pressed against hers. "We're ok," he murmured, his voice thick with emotion. He kissed Caleb's forehead. "We're okay." He then kissed Ivy's forehead. "We're okay."

* * *

GREYSON

Back at the house, Grey stood in front of his mother, his fists clenched at his sides. His eyes burned with anger, the tension in the room thick enough to cut through.

"You were her grandmother for ten years," he began, his voice low and cold. "You got to be a part of Ivy's life because of your lies. But because of you, Lily's mother never had that chance. She has an aunt, a wonderful woman who raised an extraordinary young man, that she'll never get to meet. That shame is on you, Mom."

His mother opened her mouth to speak, but Greyson cut her off, his voice rising. "Do you have any idea what you've done? You almost cost me my family. AGAIN!"

He could still hear the screams in his head—the kids, Lily's whimpers, all of them as they clung to each other, waiting for the storm to tear them apart. Grey had three core memories he always hoped to never add to - Lily's empty hospital bed, Ivy hooked up to more machines than she had body space for and seeing his fellow Marines blow apart, burning alive. Now, because of his mother, he had a fourth-

living through his family almost being swept away in a fucking tornado.

"And for what?" his voice broke. "To fuel some sick need to be right all the time? To have me to yourself? Lily was going to leave me. Again. Because of you, because my stupid ass thought there might be something, somewhere, redeemable in you. That maybe you'd learned something in the ten years of lying, scheming, and manipulating us. That maybe you'd made a monstrous mistake and were simply too scared to get yourself out from under it...But you *enjoyed* this all the way until our children were in the path of a tornado. And honestly, I'm not even sure if it was Ivy you cared about or yourself."

Her face paled, but Greyson didn't stop. "You're my mother, so I'm going to give you more courtesy than I would give anyone else who pulled an *eighth* of what you've pulled. Man or beast, I would have given you your wings. Because you are my mother, today you get to leave here with your life. I don't want to see you again and if I do, I will deal with you like any stranger on the street who endangered my family."

The finality of his words hung in the air, a death sentence. And for the first time, his mother seemed to understand the gravity of what she had done.

"Son, I–"

Grey made a slashing motion with his hand, silencing her.

Without another word, she turned and walked out, leaving behind the wreckage of her manipulation and lies. As the door closed behind her, Greyson let out a shaky breath. The storm had passed, but the damage remained.

And now, they had to figure out how to rebuild.

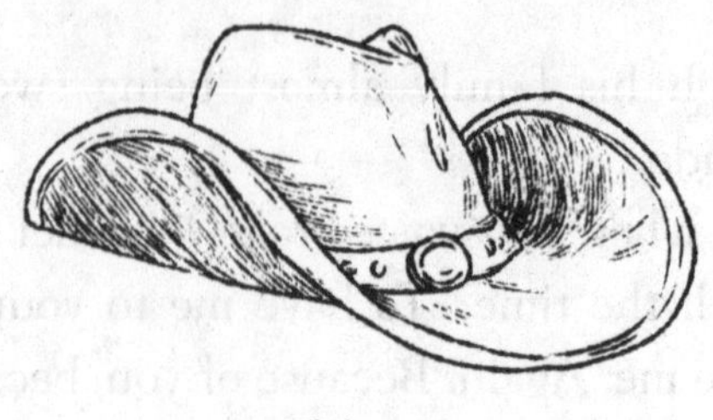

14

GREAT IDEA

"THIS IS A *GREAT* IDEA," LILY MOANED INTO HIS EAR AS she rode him soft and sweet. They had tucked themselves away in the loft of one of the outbuildings and were making love for the second time that afternoon.

With their kids and the students off on a field trip to Silver Creek Ranch, Lily and Grey were taking some much needed time to reconnect.

"Give me that pretty mouth, Songbird," Grey demanded. Her sweet, full lips landed on his and he got lost in her even more. They drank each other in, took, and gave until neither could move.

"Gotta get your chest out of the sun," Lily mumbled into his arm. "Sun's strong through the skylight."

"UV reinforced baby," he said with a yawn, kissing her on the top of her head. "Thank you for thinking of me."

She always make sure he protected his grafts, always turning his moisturizer routine into another way for them to connect with slow strokes and gentle kisses. She was still the kind, thoughtful soul who just made it easier to exist in the world.

"I know we are focused on building something new, Songbird, but I have to say I fucking hated my life without you. Ivy was my one bright spot. I poured love into her, bled dedication to the Corps... I had more to give. Loving you is my thank you to God for allowing me to see another day."

Her eyelashes fluttered against his chest, tickling him a bit. "Just when I think you've said all the sweet things you could ever say, you find new ways to make me fall in love with you all over again." She squeezed him tight, sliding a leg over his.

"Do you think you could fall in love with me again for the rest of our lives?"

Lily sat up to get a close look at him. "What?"

Grey reached a long arm to his hastily discarded pants and fumbled with the pocket, producing a small, cream velvet box. "Open."

Lily smiled. "Me or the box?"

He tucked a curl behind her ear and raised a brow. "The box in my hand first."

Her giggles washed over him, settling in him deep. A gasp followed. "Grey, baby."

"A different ring for a new beginning," he said, taking the emerald-cut diamond ring out of the box and showing her the inscription on the inside - an anchor, a piece of ivy, and little bear.

Lily laughed through her tears. "For ten years you hated the song and now this?"

"For ten years, I thought you were singing about a love triangle."

"What?!"

"'*From two, to three, baby, we were meant to be, cause I'm anchored to you.*'"

Lily fell back on the blankets, clutching the ring to her chest, her laughter rocking her body. Grey gently pried open her hand, slipping the ring out and guiding it onto her finger.

"From two to four, baby forever more. I'm anchored to you."

EPILOGUE

Lily was in the kitchen, brewing a cup of chamomile tea, when she heard the soft sound of footsteps approaching. Ivy wandered in; her expression closed and uncomfortable. Lily zeroed in on her daughter's fingers twisting the ring Lily gave her made from ashes of her affable grandfather.

"Hey, Sweetheart," she said, concern filling her voice. "What's up?"

Ivy shuffled her feet, fidgeting with the hem of her shirt. "Um, can I talk to you about something?"

Lily put down her mug, her heart racing. She would never take for granted these moments with her baby. She put a lock on her enthusiasm and focused on her girl. "Of course! You can tell me anything." She motioned for Ivy to come closer, and the young girl sat at the kitchen island, her eyes downcast.

"I got my period," Ivy said quietly, the words barely escaping her lips.

Lily felt a wave of empathy wash over her. This

moment felt monumental. She remembered the awkwardness she'd felt at Ivy's age, the blend of fear, dread with a touch of excitement. "Okay," she replied gently, making her way to Ivy's side. "That's completely normal. It can be a little scary at first, but I promise it's something every girl goes through."

Ivy nodded, but her brow furrowed in concern. "This sucks. I'm the first girl I know to get it."

Lily placed a reassuring hand on Ivy's back, rubbing it softly. "I got mine kinda early too. At my eleventh birthday party wearing my brand new, cute pink jeans and matching jacket. I got off my bike and left a stain on the seat."

"Oh NO!"

"Oh. Yes." I wanted to crawl under a rock, but it wasn't long before I was the girl everyone came to when they got theirs instead of going to the nurse. Momma thought I was hemorrhaging, I was going through too many pads in a month!"

Ivy laughed hard and Lily reached out to cup her face. "You'll get the hang of it, and it'll be days that it sucks more than others, but I can help you with that."

"Dad is going to go overboard," Ivy admitted, a hint of exasperation in her voice. "I got a slide deck on The Human Body and Procreation when I turned ten. It was like he was planning a mission."

Lily chuckled softly and nodded. "That sounds like him, but know he goes all in because he loves you."

Ivy nodded, her face relaxing a little. "Yeah, I know. Thanks Momma."

Every time.

Every time her baby called her 'Mom' or 'Momma' or even 'Mo-om' in annoyance her heart stuttered a bit.

Every. Single. Time. And she'd take a thousand mini-heart attacks as long as she could keep hearing it.

"Thanks for not making it weird," Ivy said softly.

"I'll leave that up for your dad, and here he is now."

Grey came around the corner looking from Lily to Ivy with a wide smile on his face. After forehead kisses for his girls, he waited for one of them to say something.

"Don't make it weird," Ivy said.

"Ivy got her period," Lily said.

Grey stood frozen for a minute then blinked. "I've got it all ready for you." He turned and took off toward the hallway closet.

"He's going to make it weird."

"Yep," Lily said, taking her daughter's hand with one and sipping her tea with the other.

Grey rushed back into the room with two boxes.

"Your first period pack and your go bag," he announced.

The first box was sizeable and Lily busted out laughing. "Um... how many pads did you buy?!"

"And when did you do all this?" Ivy said as she looked horrified.

"When you turned ten," Grey said with a mild attitude. "You stay ready so you don't have to get ready." He started pulling everything out of the big box and the more he pulled out the more she fell in love with him.

The man had thought of everything. He pulled out a selection of pads, tampons, period panties in various sizes, menstrual cups and caps so that Ivy could find what she was most comfortable with. He bought a heating pad, a warm fuzzy blanket that looked like a burrito tortilla, comfy sweats, and thick, fuzzy socks. There were teas and giftcards for local restaurants, pain medicine, a couple journals, pretty pens, face masks, and little stuffed uterus with a frowny face on one side and happy face on the other.

It was phenomenal and by the time he finished Lily and Ivy were both bawling.

"Thank you, Daddy," she said as she hugged him tight.

Lily followed right behind her, "That was amazing, you're amazing."

Caleb wandered into the kitchen, took in the teary women and the various menstrual cycle matter and groaned.

"Oh no...did they sync up?" He shook his head, grabbed an apple, and beat a hasty retreat out the back door.

* * *

LILY SAT on the edge of her bed, the morning breeze filtering through the curtains giving her goosebumps. It had been six months since the surgery to repair her voice—a procedure that brought both hope and anxiety. She hadn't spoken a word since the day she'd undergone the operation, choosing to communicate through American Sign Language or writing things down. Today she was going to find out if it worked.

As she wrapped her fingers around her belly, the realization of her pregnancy settled in—a beautiful sight that brought tears to her eyes. She felt a mixture of joy and fear; what if the surgery didn't work? What if her child never heard her sing? What if she got her voice, but lost the baby? Her heartbeat sped up as anxiety coursed through her.

"Hey, Songbird," Grey called softly, studying her like he always did.

"I'm scared," she signed.

He knelt beside her. "I know," he replied and signed

back, his voice full of patience and understanding. "But you're not alone in this. We're in it together."

Lily nodded, so grateful for him and their growing family in that moment, she allowed herself to hope.

"Wait here," he said, standing up. He walked over to his phone, quickly pulling up old interviews of her singing and sharing her story. He connected it to a small speaker, a smile playing on his lips as he scrolled through the videos.

He placed the speaker gently against her belly. "This is still you," he said, his tone serious but tender. "Whatever happens, we'll make it through together."

Lily felt the warmth of his hand against her skin, and the sound of her own voice filled the room. The familiar tune wrapped around her like a comforting blanket, easing her worries some.

As the last notes faded, Greyson leaned closer. "You'll find your voice again. I believe in you. Plus, I threw six silver dollars into the fountain."

She grinned a bit and signed a question, "What if I can't?"

"Then we'll sing for," he responded, squeezing her hand reassuringly. "We'll sing for you."

* * *

MONTHS LATER, Lily stood in the middle of a small club in Los Angeles, her heart racing as the spotlight illuminated her figure. She wore a simple black turtleneck, black miniskirt, and modified high heels.

Her leg would never be what it was, the human body was not meant to withstand the impact she experienced, but the fact that she *could* walk was a miracle. She glanced down at her leg and smiled. It looked like a horror show, still. And her team...bless them. They were shocked she wouldn't cover it. They had whole lookbooks with fantastic one-legged outfits and mockups of what Hollywood movie magic could do to make her 'appear whole.'

"I'm already whole," she told a room full of record execs and handlers at the meeting. She laid out how the rest of her life as LaLa Fair would go, her modified and scaled back tour schedule, etc. They were tepidly on board until she refused to 'prove' her voice was back. She didn't have to prove shit.

So, she went with plan B, bought out her contract, and went live on social media before the ink was dry to announce her *Booked and Boozy Tour*. A stripped down, small club tour designed to connect with her fans more intimately. It was the Hen House on a Friday night, but international.

It sold out within twenty minutes. She added additional days to each stop. They sold out even faster. Her former record company regretted their haste. They would have to learn to live with it.

And so now here she was. Glasses in place. Honey blond curls instead of a platinum blowout, breast pads sewn into her bra so she didn't leak before she had time to pump after her set... Bits of Lily had always shown through LaLa's facade, and someday maybe the world would know the real her, but let's face it - LaLa was infinitely more fun. And she was ready to have fun.

Taking a deep breath, she gripped the microphone, the weight of it familiar, comforting.

Greyson stood off to the side, pride shining in his eyes as he nodded his support. She focused on Caleb and Ivy, who were standing stage right in the wings, anticipation etched on their faces, then closed her eyes and the world around her faded, leaving only love and music.

As she opened her mouth to sing, the first note erupted with a clarity she hadn't known in years. It felt as if every moment of struggle had led her to this very instance—a reclamation of her identity, her voice, and her family.

The crowd swayed, caught up in the emotion behind her lyrics. Each word carried the weight of her journey, the pain and joy woven into a story only she could sing.

Lily was stronger, brighter, and ready to release the gift inside her.

As the last note lingered in the air, she glanced at Greyson, who was clearing the wet from his eyes and she felt a sense of peace settle within her. Whatever lay ahead, they would face it together, united by love, music, and the promise of new beginnings.

Miss Grey and Lily already?
Check out the bonus scene here:
https://bit.ly/reuniterancherbonus

Want to talk about the book with other readers?
Join Terreece's Thirst Trap on Facebook:
https://bit.ly/terreecethirsttrap

Thanks for reading book four of the
Silver Creek Ranch series, don't forget to leave a review!

Up next is **The Rancher's Home** *by Darie McCoy!*
Make sure you snag book five today!

THE RANCHER'S HOME (SILVER CREEK RANCH BOOK 5)

When home isn't just a place.

Former Army Ranger Rothschild 'Roth' Stephens has found comforting peace in the vast, tranquil expanse of his Texas ranch. Scarred both physically and emotionally from his time in the service, Roth prefers his own quiet company, filling his days with the grueling, rhythmic chores of ranch life.

Autumn Daley, a successful corporate attorney, has spent years burying herself in work to escape the haunting memories of her past. However, her work life has become untenable. Circumstances bring her home where she faces old memories, along with the man who witnessed the most horrible day of her life. Roth Stephens. Her brother's best friend.

When they meet again, they both attempt to ignore their draw to one another. However, Autumn is forced to seek Roth's help. The sparks they'd tried to deny existed, ignite. What starts as a simple favor soon evolves into a deeper connection as they confront their pasts and navigate the complexities of their emotions.

Roth finds a different kind of peace with Autumn. But, can he hold on to it? What will it take for them to realize the home they seek is with each other?

Read The Rancher's Home, Book 5 in the Silver Creek Ranch Series

ALSO BY TERREECE M CLARKE

Contemporary Romance

Heartbeat

The first book in the Courageous Love Series is a deeply emotional story of love in extraordinary circumstances, developing the courage to be vulnerable after devastating life events, and the ruthlessness of one man's obsession.

Love Never

Life is meant to be experienced especially when life hands a visiting professor a biker who was as suave as his nickname "Smooth" suggested. For one weekend she allowed herself to spend 96 hours in heaven. Damn the consequences.

Chaser

A plus-sized, billionaire finds herself entangled in a sizzling friends-with-benefits affair with Xavier, a devoted cowboy businessman.

Fingertips

A rising executive and her boss's new client – a heated workplace romance that goes deeper than one night.

Breathless

The love story of Juliette and Logan (Wolf).

The Christmas War Paws

Dr. Francesca Johnson-DeWitt's post-divorce plans take an unexpected turn in the charming town of Ohio Falls where her college nemesis, the smug Dr. Sebastian Bing, rekindles an old rivalry sparking a hilarious and heartwarming Christmas War that turns the quaint town upside down.

Adult Coloring Books

Book Boyfriend Adult Coloring Book

Join my mailing list so you never miss a single release AND get behind the scenes looks and bonus scenes!

Bit.ly.com/terreecewrites

ABOUT THE AUTHOR

A native of Columbus, Ohio by way of Toledo, bestselling author and journalist Terreece M. Clarke writes about smart women experiencing extraordinary love. 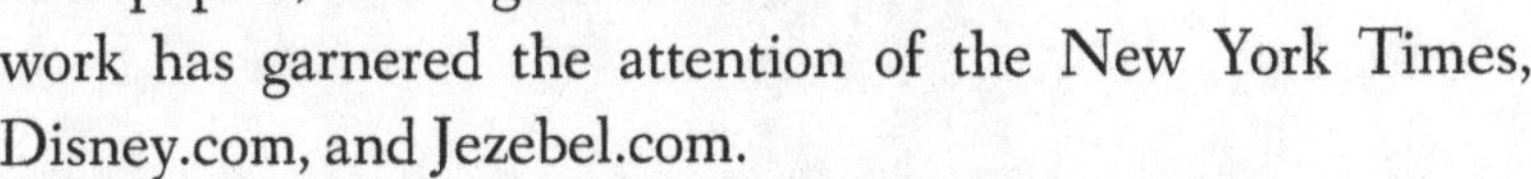

She is an advocate for those whose voices are often ignored has written for a variety of websites, magazines, newspapers, and organizations and her work has garnered the attention of the New York Times, Disney.com, and Jezebel.com.

Terreece's debut novel, Heartbeat, became a #1 Amazon international bestseller in two categories and launched the bestselling Courageous Love Series.

When she's not juggling family, she's busting a move or reading in her bubble she's on social media forwarding cute cat videos to EVERYONE. Be sure to follow her on all the socials.